THE OPIATE MURDERS 2

The River Man of Dundas Street

Justin Sand

◆ FriesenPress

One Printers Way
Altona, MB R0G 0B0
Canada

www.friesenpress.com

Copyright © 2021 by Justin Sand
First Edition — 2021

All rights reserved.

No part of this publication may be reproduced in any form, or by any means, electronic or mechanical, including photocopying, recording, or any information browsing, storage, or retrieval system, without permission in writing from FriesenPress.

ISBN
978-1-03-913084-5 (Hardcover)
978-1-03-913083-8 (Paperback)
978-1-03-913085-2 (eBook)

1. FICTION, CRIME

Distributed to the trade by The Ingram Book Company

1

THERE IS A WAREHOUSE; IT ISN'T CLOSE TO THE CITY, NOR IS IT FAR. IT resides over the highway off the road known as the Don Way in the industrial park, where the smell of iron and freight fill the air. On the third day of the third month of 2021, the legion was set to meet there. It was so dark and so quiet in that section of the city that you could hear the rats scurry from place to place. All that could be heard was the cars and trucks as they passed by on the highway.

A man limped his way up to the front of the building and knocked once upon the door. The door opened without a pause, and a large man with a ski mask let Dax in. He was given a cloak and told to follow the hallway until it opened into a large space. This was dimly lit around the edges with a blue flame burning in the middle of the room. He could see a large group of cloaked men standing in a line passing by the blue flame. He could hear the sound of breaking glass. He held his glass pipe close to his chest and took a deep breath.

It had been a long three months. Many souls had passed since he had arrived in Toronto. The weather was cold and unforgiving just like the people. He met little resistance, and his actions went unnoticed. He called them his "beautiful dozen", the four men and eight women he had collected since he had arrived. His power had increased with every kill, and his anxiety had diminished with every news broadcast. Toronto was a free-for-all. He went to the funerals. Nobody suspected a thing.

As he stood in the line, he leaned on his cane to rest his leg. He was getting old for sure, and this weather didn't agree with his joints. He could hear the clinking of glass ahead of him as he dreaded releasing his bounty. He was to relinquish his souls to Charon, who would take them across the river to the land of the dead. Charon was the leader of this outfit, and even though he was said to be young, he was already a legend. They called him the River Man of Dundas Street. He was said to have collected a thousand souls in his tenure.

It was legend that Charon's father was police and one night he was killed by a junkie in High Park. His mother, consumed by grief, had committed suicide shortly after. Charon came up in the foster-care system and eventually hit the street. His hunger for souls was insatiable. He was revered, and in time, his legend grew so big amongst the Legion that he was given his own chapter out here. Dax had come to Toronto exclusively to meet him. Tonight, would be the night.

As Dax approached the altar, he kissed the dozen and said the prayer of St. Michael. He looked into the dark chalice beside the blue flame and tossed his pipe into the abyss. He heard the glass break as it hit the rest of the sacrificial glass. Dax made his way over to the side and stood in line, arm to arm, with the other cloaked men. He watched as the others, who had formed a line behind him, dropped their sacrifices into the chalice. This was the moment he had waited for all this time.

From the back of the building, three men cloaked in black garments walked slowly forward. Two of the men stood on either side as one of them picked up the chalice and stacked it atop the blue flame above the stand that encased it. The room went dark; all that could be seen was a dim red and blue flame burning the bottom of the chalice. One of the men standing on the side smashed the glass inside the chalice with a piece of steel, and sparks flew from underneath on every impact. Smoke began to rise from the chalice and the smell of fentanyl and death filled the air.

The two men on either side of the chalice stood back as another cloaked figure stepped forward. He removed the hood from his head and stood for a second, examining the group. Two torches were lit on either side of the chalice and left to burn at a high heat. All that smoke danced in the flames of the torches and then made its way upwards. "Brothers I welcome you," said the young man suddenly. His hair was dark brown, but his eyes twinkled like diamonds of blue. He had sharp features but no sign of age upon his face. He stood there, as immaculate as a statue or a portrait.

He glared at the chalice and spoke with the reverence of a preacher. "In these last months, I have seen the future. I have seen the truth. I have seen the scourge of our city rounded up by COVID and dispersed by our hands. I have seen the trauma-ridden souls emancipated from their carcasses and urged on into the river. January 2021 saw the highest number of drug deaths in the history of our city. If they only knew, gentlemen. If they only knew. I'm so proud of the men in this room. I would like to welcome a new member tonight from the West Coast. I know he is one of the reasons we are celebrating tonight." Charon opened his hand and extended it towards Dax.

Dax raised his hand and said, "I am legion," and then every man in the room shouted, "I AM LEGION!"

"Brothers, tonight I am here to thank you. But more importantly I am here to express admiration for your talents. For too long, we have seen our streets become open sewers. For too long, our social services have become homes for enablement. I admire your courage and perseverance in being able to do the job that our weak politicians and civil servants can't do. This city's leadership is full of cowards. When I look at you tonight, I feel the pride we once had in this city returning.

"You stood up and said, 'No!' No more homeless paradise; no more junkie vacation destination. This is our city, and we will continue to send these souls back where they came from." Charon took a deep breath, and the room broke out into cheers. Smoke surrounded the altar, and they all watched as Charon put the hood back over his head and stepped forward towards the chalice. He put his hands into the smoke and bowed his head as everyone in the room reached out their arms and bowed theirs.

Charon opened both his hands and dropped two handfuls of coins into the chalice. "I take you now across the river and back to darkness. I've freed you from the chains of existence. I free you from time. In the name of St. Michael, I cast you out of paradise."

The room erupted in applause, but no other sound was heard for miles around except for that of the cars and trucks that sped down the highway.

2

AMY WINTER SAT AT HER DESK, SCROLLING THROUGH THE LATEST HEADlines that bombarded her screen. Five overdose deaths had been reported yesterday, which would set her city on its way to another historic record. She thought the last year had been bad, but now this was beginning to look like a brand-new low. She turned off her computer and stretched her back. She ran her hands down her skirt, ironing out any wrinkles and looked at the reflection of herself in the mirror adjacent her desk. She had long, blonde hair that had seen better colour, but in the winter, it went with her white complexion. Her eyes were mostly grey, but every once in a while, they would shine through blue. She had been able to stay fit through the pandemic because she ran at home, so she moved more gracefully than a lot of women in her position.

She looked at the pictures of her two kids on her desk and exhaled. She was due in the morgue to meet the new overdose victims. It was never easy, but the younger the dead were, the harder it was for her to carry on with the rest of her day. She thought after fifteen years of working in the coroner's office she would be more seasoned, but she always dreaded seeing the recently deceased, if they were young. She chalked it up to still having a heart in an industry that deals exclusively with death. She hadn't yet lost that part of herself that yearns for life.

She looked out her window into that dreary Ontario March weather and shuttered. She put on her coat and headed for the basement. As she walked to the elevator, she kept her head down. She had a lot on her mind and wasn't interested in small talk, especially with other government workers. There were only so many kids, photos, and cabins-up-north-renovation stories she could hear. As the elevator reached the basement, she stepped out and adjusted her game face as she walked into the back of a very large room with steel tables lining the edges.

She was met by Ahmed, the team lead on the morgue floor. He motioned to the five tables in the far, right corner of the room. "Good morning," she said as Ahmed finished what he was doing and approached the first bed.

"Good morning, Amy. So, this is the first," he said as he pulled back the sheet "found off of Dundas early this morning, late fifties, no known residence. We are still working on his identity. He had a mixture of fentanyl, benzo, and the new stuff xylazine."

Amy nodded as Ahmed pulled the sheet back over the pale, blue-lipped corpse. He then proceeded to show Amy the rest of the bodies; all late forties to sixties, all homeless, all without identities. Amy exhaled as she felt the relief come back to her. *No dead kids.* Just then, she was interrupted by a thought. "So, it was too late for all of them?" she asked, insinuating that the paramedics had delivered them all DOA to the hospital.

"No, that's the part that is bothering me the most," Ahmed said as he stepped to the middle table. "These last three didn't respond to Narcan, and they died on route."

"Seriously?" Amy asked as she rubbed her forehead.

"This combination of drugs is leaving people with no defence," Ahmed confirmed in dismay.

Amy was beginning to see this outcome more and more among the homeless population. The dope wasn't mixed with enough fentanyl to be susceptible to Narcan, and the new drug Xylazine put them in a coma where they would suffocate to death. If you added the complication of COVID protocols into the mix, these people didn't stand a chance. The camps made things even more grave. Since the beginning of the pandemic, homeless camps had been popping up all over the city, and tent checks were revealing dead bodies in the morning. So now, even if you got to the person on time and the paramedics were already geared up with PPE, the person still died because the Narcan didn't take. This was a nightmare. There were 120 camps spread throughout the city along major routes, and every day, people on those routes would die from overdoses.

Amy looked at Ahmed. "Thank you, I look forward to your report," was all she said.

That was all she could say. She looked at those reports every day. It started with the paramedic report and then funneled down the line. She read the police report if there was one, and then the autopsy if they did one. The bodies were buried in mass graves outside of the city. Amy shook her head and got ready for her briefing with the mayor. She didn't get surprised anymore by the way things were handled. Everyone's hands were tied; she knew that.

3

MIKAH SAT AT HER STATION, WATCHING PEOPLE BEING USHERED INTO THE safe injection site on Victoria Street. She remembered back to her job interview. "How would you feel if people tell you to 'fuck off' to your face?" was one of the questions. She had answered, "Well, I guess it depends on the situation." She was then presented with the next question: "What if the person tells you to fuck off every time they see you, and you see them five times a day?"

She had already lasted three weeks, which was a surprise even to herself. She had just graduated from the University of Toronto with a BA in psychology. She figured she should get some experience before she pursued her master's degree. She couldn't possibly get a job in her field, so she took any job that she could in the social service sector. Harm reduction was willing to take her on with no experience, in the hope that she would take what she learned and spread it throughout the paradigm.

Just then, her thought process was interrupted by two participants coming in hot, screaming at each other and anyone else.

"Don't be such a goof about it!"

"Who you calling a goof? You rat bitch!"

Mikah had come to recognize the first voice as K-ultra and the other as Tdot. Mikah only knew people's site names. K-ultra sat as far away from Tdot as possible, even though the two of them spent every waking moment together. Tdot was carrying two large garbage bags, a backpack, and another bag in his hand. Mikah was going to ask him if he was moving in as a joke but quickly changed her mind, as everywhere he went, he carried his whole life on his back.

"I've been waiting all morning to do a smash! How come you guys don't open earlier?" he asked as he pulled back the three jackets he wore, revealing his slender arms and forward arching neck with four or five necklaces around it.

"I don't know," Mikah said, hoping that answer would suffice.

"Well, I'll tell ya, I'm never using outside again. Did you hear about what happened yesterday? Five people died. Five people! Three of them didn't even respond to Narcan – that's how fucked-up the dope is out there. Never again!" Tdot said as held a cooker up in front of his face and lit the bottom with a lighter.

"Oh, shut up! You always say that, and then you're like, 'C'mon forget about all that.'" K-ultra returned from his booth across the room.

"Fuck you! I mean it this time," Tdot said.

"Listen guys, check your dope here and everywhere. We aren't immune. Don't you remember what happened last year? Fourteen people OD'd in here in one day from fucked-up dope," said a voice resonating from behind the computer. Perry was the closest thing there to a mentor for Mikah. He appreciated her for just what she was: young, innocent, and willing to learn, something of a rare bird around there.

Most of the people at the safe injection site treated Mikah like she didn't belong there because she didn't come from addiction or the street. Perry knew that Mikah was from the Philippines, and in her country, they shot drug addicts. The society that Mikah came from made Toronto look like a cake walk, but she never rubbed it in anyone's face or talked down to people; she just did her job and tried to learn. Perry knew all this because his wife was from Iran, where all the same rules applied to drug addicts and similar types. His wife was just happy to be in this country, and that was something he admired about people from other countries. People from other backgrounds and countries saw Canada for what it was – paradise.

"What's immune mean?" Tdot asked finally.

"It means safe, you moron!" K-ultra yelled from his side of the room.

"Fuck off, cunt," Tdot said as he did a smash.

The room was sort of quiet for the next couple minutes. Mikah was learning to rise and fall with the waves of energy that were thrown at her every day.

"Can I get a glass of water?" Tdot said finally.

Just as Mikah got back with his water, she saw Perry stand up and walk over behind K-ultra, while putting his surgical gloves on. Perry put a hand on each shoulder and gave K-ultra a light massage until his eyes opened.

"Hey, thanks," K-ultra said as he looked around in a semi-dazed state.

Mikah had learned to walk around the room and watch people's breathing patterns and body postures. Leaning back wasn't good nor was leaning too far forward. They didn't want people sleeping, so the game being played was one of touch and go. When a client nodded off, they were immediately touched on the shoulder to get their eyes open, especially right after they used. Sometimes this was done multiple times. After a while, it became easy to tell what was sleeping, what was nodding, and what was overdosing.

When a participant was done in the gallery, they went into observation, a room where they could go if they still wanted to be observed. Some slept, some coloured, and others played guitar. "The dope babysits them," Perry told her on her first day. "If we can get them through the waiting room and into a booth, then they are okay. Everything else is madness. Once they are high, they go back to their original state. Well, unless they smash crystal or something like that. Then they are dancing in the booth and running from one side of the room to another, sweating, talking, and having a party. People come here to party," he said.

Mikah and the team worked twelve-hour shifts in a place where people from all walks of life came in to use dope. It was an adjustment for her, to say the least.

"Hey Joe, you alright over there?" Perry yelled across the room to the last booth on the right. Joe's head had cocked back, and his eyes were shut tight.

"He better not be going down. Fuck off, Joe. Don't try to ruin my high," Tdot said, yelling over in Joe's direction.

Perry motioned to Mikah to grab the oxygen tank and the pre-ready shots on the counter, and the two of them moved behind Joe quickly. Perry rubbed Joe's shoulders, but he wasn't responding. Just then, Sandra came out of the observation room to assist them. "Okay, let's lean him back," Perry said in a calm voice. The three of them leaned the chair back all the way until Joe was on the ground on his back. Sandra put the oxygen on his face as Perry checked the pulse. "Mikah, I want you to give him a shot in the leg."

Mikah took the pre-drawn Narcan needle out of the kit. Her hands were shaking, but she took the lid off the needle and held it as steady as she could. Perry reached under Joe's leg and squeezed his hamstring. Mikah hesitantly poked the needle into the semi-taut quad that Perry had made visible for her and pressed the plunger down until she heard the vanishing edge retract back into the syringe. Sandra immediately gave Joe another shot in the other leg.

"Okay, time two minutes," Perry said as he rubbed Joe's shoulders. Mikah's heart was pounding as she held Joe's hand. A minute later, Joe's eyes opened to the sound of applause. "Welcome back, my friend," Perry said in a soft voice. "Can we stand you up?"

Joe rose to his feet with the help of Sandra and Mikah. "Rest here a while. You gotta take it easy, Joe," Sandra said as she went back into observation with Tdot trailing her.

"Thanks a lot, asshole," Tdot said as he followed Sandra into the other room.

"It's okay, Joe," K-ultra rattled off in his semi-conscious state.

"Fill out the report," Perry said to Mikah. "Was that your first one?" he asked, patting her shoulder.

"First one I've Narcan'd, but I've assisted many times." Mikah was jacked. Her heart was pounding and a feeling of euphoria filled her being as she tried to sit still and fill out the report on the computer.

"Make sure you report the stat. We don't want our funding cut," Perry scoffed. He patted Joe on the back and then went to sit back down.

K-ultra was alert now too, adjusting his things and holding a small baggy up to the light above him. Everything settled right down after that. It was like a cool breeze had run through the unit on a hot day.

Once Mikah had filled out the report, she walked across the street to Tim Hortons to get a coffee. She couldn't hold the world close enough after that. Her first save! She felt like she was on top of the world. She had all sorts of fears that the needle was going to bend or that it wouldn't go through the jeans, but all that dissolved when the needle went through like butter. It was effortless. Her arms tingled from the experience. She couldn't shake the warm feeling that engulfed her.

Holding Joe's hand was something she learned early on. "You want the human touch, so the person knows where to come back to. Some say it's the Narcan, but we think it takes more than that," she had been told. She felt tremendous as she walked back across the street with her coffee. She felt for the first time in her life that she belonged to this earth and was a manifestation of it. Like a rose in full bloom. She drank her coffee outside for a few moments and gathered herself. When she stepped back in the unit all she could hear was yelling.

"If I don't get my shoes back, I'm going to kill someone," said a voice from the observation room.

She was back, and the feeling slipped into the background as she welcomed a couple of new participants. "Whose stuff is this in this booth? I'm trying to get high. This isn't a garage sale," the man said.

"Touch my shit and die," Tdot yelled from the next room.

Perry yelled back, "One room or the other Tdot," to which K-ultra yelled "Ya, you goof" then Tdot came steaming back into the room to his booth. "Fuck you, cunt," he said as he passed K-ultra. "Watch out, guy. Joe Joe just went down on that shit," Tdot told the new guy, Mark45.

Mark45 turned and said, "I can handle my dope, just watch me." He did a smash standing up in a matter of minutes and walked out of the unit saying, "That's how it's done; doesn't take me all day."

Mikah looked to the clock. It said 12:30 p.m. She still had 9.5 hours to go.

4

A WOMAN PUSHED HER CART DOWN QUEEN STREET EAST TOWARDS Bellwood Park singing: "He takes your pain, and when he's done with you, you'll never be seen again." The whispers of death filled the ears of every street walker in the city. They all flocked to popular camps that were full of people. Like gazelles, they felt safer in the middle of the herd.

Dax sat at a bus stop listening to the woman as she walked by. He laughed to himself. "You can't stop the plague that is coming." He usually sat around the periphery of the camps and waited. Late at night, between 3:00 to 4:30 a.m., was the sweet spot. Police did a shift change and finished up their paperwork around then. It was easy to dose people then.

Dax would just sell his dope cheap for a week until he was trusted, and then he would peg off the weakest of the herd. A woman by herself was preferable, but he would take older men out on their own too. It was easy to pick off the ones out on their own. Usually, they had stolen from someone in the camp to get the money for the drugs, so they wouldn't be missed anyway. It was all too easy, except for the cold. Dax's joints killed from the cold. He wasn't used to it; -1° maybe, but not this -10° to -20° shit.

Dax lit a cigarette. *Maybe I should head down to the east and find a hooker. These homeless are too easy. I need a thrill,* he thought. Just as he was about to leave, he saw her. She couldn't have been older than twenty and was walking down the street with a huge duffle bag attached to her back. His eyes lit up with a flash of euphoria. *The hunt was sweeter than the kill* was all he could see or understand. He stayed behind her as she walked and stayed out of sight when she stopped. She was aware of danger, but she couldn't see it. She sensed it but couldn't locate it. She continued on, past the camp and behind a school. She stopped there and took out her tent. She would stay there tonight. As she started setting up, she heard a sound. The snapping of a branch maybe? She scanned the field surrounding her and dismissed it for a raccoon or other night crawler. She knew she was better off alone out there, but tonight she questioned her judgement. Once she was set up, she crawled in quickly to get warm. She gripped the pepper spray in one hand and an air horn in the other. She was so tired. All she wanted to do was sleep. She could hear the sound of traffic; she could smell the winter receding into spring. She fell asleep there all alone behind the school.

Dax sat out beyond the periphery and watched. He watched until the darkness had a hint of light. He saw the line he would take to the tent and got his gear ready. He slowly made his way out from behind his blind and crept towards the tent. Once he was right beside it, he cut a very small hole in the roof and shoved a plastic tube in it. He sprayed his concoction through the tube, filling the tent. Once he reached the limit, he pulled the tube out and crept back to his blind.

He waited… and waited. The sky started to turn light blue. He came out of the blind and walked directly up to the tent. As he walked by, he swiped the tent with his cane as hard as he could. Nothing moved… "Stupid bitch," he said as made his way to the road and into the morning sun. He felt invigorated in the morning sun dancing against his skin with the thought of another wiped from the slate. He would await the morning news, like music to his ears. His purpose shining for all to see, but no one to know but him. He lived for these moments. They made the years disappear, the joints warm and young again. The sun illuminated his walk home.

He felt his end coming soon. "Please soon," he asked the morning sun as he disappeared somewhere off of East Dundas Street.

5

THE HEADLINE ON THE FRONT PAGE OF THE *TORONTO STAR* READ: "15-year-old girl found dead from drug asphyxiation in a tent outside St. Mary's Elementary School." It was a feeding frenzy. Amy was bombarded with calls for details from the mayor's office, MP's, and even the premier. She was front and center on this.

Amy couldn't look at the pictures on her desk as she took her last sip of coffee and went down to the morgue. She didn't have to avoid eye contact on her way down because everyone avoided eye contact with her. When the doors opened, she made her way into the large room with the bright halogen lights. Ahmed finished up talking to a number of members on his team in his office and then came out to meet Amy. "Hello" was all he said as he led Amy past the stainless-steel tables and into the holding room.

Amy took a deep breath as Ahmed opened the door and pulled the body out of the wall on its steel mortuary table. "Ready?" Ahmed said as he looked at Amy.

"Yes," Amy said automatically without thinking.

He slid the sheet off of the body and revealed a pale, white girl with strawberry blonde hair. She looked much younger than fifteen as she lay there exposed to the world. "We found traces of marijuana under her fingernails. The tox screen shows a heavy dose of xylazine, etizolam (benzo), and fentanyl," Ahmed said.

"Anything else?" Amy asked putting her hand up to her cheek and resting her head on it.

"She has a bruise here. It's postmortem. You can see by the discoloration on the shoulder," Ahmed said pointing to it.

"So, what happened? She died sitting up and then fell to her side?" Amy asked.

"Possibly, but this kind of bruise looks like it's from a blunt-force object. I see it all the time with abuse victims," Ahmed replied.

"Thank you," Amy said, motioning for him to put the sheet back on her and close the door. "I look forward to your report," was all she said as she made her way through the morgue and out the door into the hallway. Tears were showing in her eyes when she got back to the office. "Hold my calls," Amy said as she shut the door to her office.

The coroner's job, amongst other things, has to try to put the victim's last day together. Cynthia Price, better known to her friends as "C", was a fifteen-year-old girl who had been in and out of the system since she was ten. Her mother had resorted to getting her locked up in city cells by police for the last two months. The mother did not have custody, but the grandmother did. Grandma had a noncontact order against C when she died. C had been hiding from the police for a number of weeks when they found her dead in a tent at her old elementary school.

Her last day was catalogued on a number of social media sites, but she didn't have a phone – as many homeless don't. She resorted to going online in libraries and coffee shops when she could. Her movements weren't tracked. Friends would report later that C stayed away from large encampments because that is how she was arrested by the police the first time. C had a history of drug use and love trysts with men far older than she was. She was reported as just another casualty in the opiate epidemic sweeping the country.

6

"YOU SEE THAT GIRL ON THE NEWS? I KNEW THAT GIRL!" TDOT SAID AS HE slammed his backpack into the booth at the safe injection site.

"Yeah, you tried to date her, and she told you to fuck off, you weirdo," K-ultra said, coming in behind him.

"Can you morons shut up!" Cristy yelled at them, and they both fell silent. She had been trying to find a vein for an hour, but she couldn't find it. Mikah couldn't watch anymore. The table in front of Cristy was full of blood and rigs. Tears streamed from Cristy's eyes as she unpackaged another rig and looked at herself in the mirror. Cristy's dad had been shot in front of her by the police when she was fourteen, and she had been in and out of foster homes and older men's beds ever since.

Her boyfriend Mikey was in observation. They weren't allowed to be in the same room inside the unit. They fought like lunatics if they were. She would punch and bite him repeatedly, refusing to let him go. "I give her hundreds of dollars of dope a day, and she can't find a vein anymore. She always wants more, and if I don't give it to her, she attacks," he would say in dismay in the next room. When they started screaming at each other, all the air was sucked out of the room. They took the whole place hostage. Everyone would pack up and leave. "Fuck you, you goof!" Cristy would scream at him. "Fuck you, hooker" he would return, and it would go on from there. Now they had to be separated.

Mikah had never seen anything like it. These two would go from leaning on each other and nodding off one minute to trying to devour each other the next. "Lovers in a dangerous time," Perry said as he looked up from the newspaper. "Sometimes he gets arrested on purpose, so he can get locked up, so they can have a break." Perry followed with a sigh.

"I believe it," Mikah said.

Just then, Cristy stood up and screamed and threw the rig at the mirror and ran out the door. Mikah's adrenalin spiked, and she started to take deep beaths.

"Good, that bitch is crazy," Tdot said. "So anyway, I knew that girl they found the other day," Tdot continued, shifting in his chair and leaving the needle in his arm to dangle back and forth. "I think she was taken," Tdot followed.

"Fuck off with that taken shit," K-ultra said.

"What's taken?" Mikah asked.

"Sometimes people just disappear, especially lately. I mean so many people are gone, just disappeared," Tdot said.

"How can she be taken if they found her in a tent, dummy?" K-ultra said, doing a smash and sitting back as he threw the rig on the table with two fingers and exhaled.

"I don't know," Tdot said, pulling the rig out of his arm.

Mikah cringed when he did it. The mirrors in the booths allowed you to see everything from the desk.

"Then she wasn't taken," K-ultra said.

"Who is taking these people?" Mikah asked.

"Fucking ghosts," Tdot said under his breath.

"Don't fucking say it! Let's go, idiot. You are ruining my high," K-ultra said as he smacked Tdot in the back of the head, and they both left.

"What is that all about?" Mikah asked.

Perry exhaled and leaned forward, looking down at the ground. "Since last year, people have been going missing, sometimes four a week, never to be found."

"Where do they go?" Mikah said wide eyed and concerned.

"The hope is that they go home to their families or out to the West Coast, but I'm not sure anymore," Perry said folding up the paper and throwing it on the desk.

"Why?" Mikah asked.

"There's just too many," Perry replied.

7

A BODY WAS FOUND FLOATING FACE DOWN IN THE KEATING CHANNEL, JUST beneath the Cherry Street lift bridge on Sunday. It wasn't on the front page; it was somewhere past page 15. Amy looked at the pathology report and saw that he had overdosed on a high level of xylazine, etizolam, and fentanyl, but how he ended up in the Don River was a mystery to her. As she flipped through the report, she noticed a note made that two coins were found in the deceased's throat. This man was a known drug trafficker and pimp. Some would say that the city was better off without him, but she had to see for herself. She asked Ahmed if he had a moment to discuss his findings, and he said he could meet her outside in an hour for coffee to discuss it.

An hour later, Ahmed found Amy sitting outside in the park with two double doubles. "Fancy meeting you here," he said with a laugh. "And thank you for the coffee."

"So, what's with the coins in the scumbag's throat?" Amy asked.

"I don't know. It's a very old ritual that nobody does anymore," Ahmed said, taking a big sip off the coffee.

"Like the old Irish ritual? I thought they had to be put over the eyes?" she asked whimsically.

"The ritual is to pay the river man to safely take the soul across the River Styx to the land of the dead," he said looking over at her.

"Sorry, I'm not up on my medieval history," she said with a laugh.

"Well, it's not medieval. It's older than that; it's Greek mythology. Charontas was the son of the night. He was the angel of death. You paid him what was called an obol to transport your soul safely across the river to the land of the dead or your body would twist in limbo and on this plain for eternity." he followed.

"So, no big deal then?" she said with a laugh. Amy took a sip of her coffee and then went into the real question. "So, the guy overdoses, and the people or person he is with pops two coins in his mouth and then pushes him into the river?"

"Well, the water has carried away any trace evidence of where this could have happened, and if he was moved, but yeah, possibly," Ahmed returned.

"Weird but not impossible that it was just a sendoff by someone who didn't want to deal with the consequences. This guy must have had a thousand enemies," Amy said.

"The coins though," Ahmed said.

"Yeah, you said they were old?" Amy returned.

"They were drachmas – Greek drachmas -- that were discontinued when the euro came in in 2001," Ahmed said.

"So, this is some kind of signature of a planned homicide using drugs?" Amy mused.

"Possibly," Ahmed said.

"I'll look through the police report to see what they had. It was pretty thin from what I saw. A guy walking his dog by the bridge on Sunday saw the body. No witnesses to the dumping. Nobody reported the victim missing. Real thin," Amy said with a sigh. "Well, thank you for your time today, sir."

"Thanks for the coffee," Ahmed said as he walked ahead of Amy back to the morgue.

Amy stood outside and looked up at the tall buildings that surrounded her work. "The River Styx in Toronto," she said to herself as she downed the last drop of coffee.

8

MIKAH SAT AT THE DESK, ABSORBING EVERYTHING SHE HEARD AND SAW since she had first learned about the missing people from the homeless population. She overheard people talking about it. Everyone knew at least three people missing. Sometimes those names overlapped, and sometimes they were cancelled out by someone reporting a sighting. It's not like people are kept track of in a database. It was all rumors and word of mouth.

The only thing that was tracked around her work was supplies, participants, and overdoses. "Keeping that funding coming our way," as Perry said. Their non-profit organization ran off funding from one place: the $4.2 billion budget allocated to the health authority. So now instead of people lining their pockets with money, they were lining their pockets with funding. This meant that each non-profit was competing with other non-profits for funding, just like in the market. Instead of six companies competing to make a better light bulb like in the market, stealing each other's secrets, employees, and not talking to each other- the non-profits competed with each other for funding providing the same service. Except that the product they were trying to create didn't involve innovation it involved helping people and that requires cooperation.

Mikah learned firsthand from watching how non-profits actively competed and didn't communicate with each other that they weren't interested in ending anything. The system was driven by funding: the less funding received by a non-profit, the less it could do, until it disappeared. Just like with capital market revenue. Revenue equaled funding, and funding meant an increase in action; in her case at the safe injection site that meant overdoses. The place was driven by overdose stats. The stats proved their usefulness. The same crossed over into every other service.

The shelters were driven by occupancy rates. Emergency services were driven by keeping people in a continuous state of emergency. Solutions weren't even sought because the model was based on volume – not eradication of the problem itself. If the problem is solved, the system collapses, so employees fought for their own survival. Mikah learned to pay homage to the stats and keep her head down. Jobs were hard to find for new people in the industry, and now she knew why.

9

MIKAH WAS ON HER BREAK, WAITING FOR HER COFFEE IN THE TIM Hortons across the street from her work. She heard her drink called out, so she walked up and grabbed the order, but just as she did, another young man approached the bar. "Sorry was that yours?" Mikah asked, blushing a little. For once she was happy to be wearing a mask so he couldn't tell.

"Yeah, but now that you've touched it, the least you can do is wait with me," he said, looking at her with the most intense blue eyes. She instantly thought of diamonds when she saw them, and she couldn't move.

"So, do you go to Ryerson too?" he said after an awkward silence.

She was still standing there looking straight towards the bar. "No, I work in the health building across the street. I went to U of T," she said reflexively, still not really used to being employed. She felt the need to tell people she had a job and where she went to school.

"Oh, what part? I have some friends who work on the third floor," he said collecting his coffee from the counter and following her outside.

"I work on the ground floor," she said looking down as she said it. Just then, he removed his mask to take a sip of his coffee. It had been a long time since she had talked to a man that attractive. She kept looking at his lips and the sharp features of his jawline and nose. The young man looked like a sculpture. She removed her mask just so she could breathe better. She sipped on her coffee awkwardly and tried to look away, but she couldn't. He was talking to her, but she didn't really catch what he said.

"So, would you like to go?" he said to her and Mikah snapped back into it.

"Where?"

"For a walk on your day off? Sorry my name is Charles."

Mikah looked back at him and said, "Yes," without really thinking. They exchanged numbers.

As Mikah walked across the street, she heard a voice yell, "Hey!" She turned and looked. "What's your name?" Charles yelled.

"It's Mikah," she said, turning crimson red. She turned quickly and walked towards the unit.

When she got in the doors, there was pandemonium inside the unit. Two people were lying on the ground and one in the observation room. Mikah quickly fell to her knees and started making Narcan shots for her coworkers, who were frantically working on the bodies. Three at once!? She had left because it was quiet. What happened?

But she had no time to think or ask. Just then, the lights from the ambulance flashed at the front doors and the paramedics came through the door. Mikah put a shot in the man lying closest to her on the ground and immediately started making another. The paramedics moved in around the others and started fixing oxygen to the man Mikah was working on. Before the situation was done, Mikah had administered three shots herself of the eight that the man beneath her took, along with the nasal dose, which was the equivalent to ten shots.

All three people were taken to the hospital, and none of them opened their eyes. Mikah had heard about things like this, but she had never seen it. She looked at Perry in the observation room, wiping the sweat from his forehead, so she could have some point of reference. However, he seemed to look right through her. She picked up her coffee off the ground, sat down, and collected herself as she watched one of the ambulances drive away.

"That must have been some crazy shit," Tdot said from the corner of the room. "Wish I had some," he followed. Mikah turned and looked at him, for the first time realizing he was there.

"Shut up, goof!" K-ultra yelled from the other side of the room.

Mikah took a sip of her coffee and adjusted herself in her chair. It didn't feel real. She was proud of herself and scared for the people on the stretchers. "Make sure you fill out the report," was all she heard from Perry as he came into the room. Mikah nodded, checking her phone for the time. It was then that she saw Charles' number on her screen.

It was now 2:15, so the first one must have been right after she left at 1:45. All that in thirty minutes!? *What a crazy job,* she thought. She didn't think about the number again as she pieced together the details from all of the people involved. The first person went down in observation, and then the other two, like dominoes, in consumption. That's when she came in. She shook her head in disbelief. She felt terrified and elated and bounced back and forth between the two extremes until she settled at a new baseline. She was pumped. She liked it. It was terrifying to be on edge like that all the time, but she liked it. Time just dissolved along with all her petty problems and grievances. She was free of the trappings of the world and immersed in the line between life and death. It had never been so close for her. It was right beneath her feet.

10

ACROSS TOWN, AROUND THE SAME TIME, HUNDREDS OF PEOPLE GATHERED for a teenage girl's funeral. Everyone was there; TV, newspapers, and even the mayor. Dax watched it all from across the street. Crowds surrounded the church in order to give their respects, huge lines of social-distanced people up and down Bathurst Street outside St. Mary's parish. Dax got to relive the whole experience. He was taken back to the moment he first saw the girl making her way up Queen Street. She was so alert, so strong. She was the perfect target, his greatest prize. He listened across the street and could hear the condolences passed on to the family as they left the building. He saw the guilt-filled and grief-ridden mother. He relished these moments.

"Now you see," he said to himself as he looked at the woman's tear-swept face. *Now you understand,* he thought as he lit a cigarette and enjoyed the show. "Can't you see she is in a better place now," he said to himself. "Can't you see what you made her become," he said glaring across the street.

His vindication resounded deep within. He was smiling from ear to ear, but he had his skeleton mask wrapped around his face, so nobody knew. He soaked up their sadness and used it to fuel his next rampage. "Bye bye, sweet darling," he whispered as he made his way down Bathurst and back to Queen. He couldn't hold the world close enough to him. He felt as if his purpose and value had been restored on this lovely spring day.

11

AMY SORTED THROUGH THE FILES ON HER COMPUTER THAT CONTAINED statistics coming out of the suburbs. The suburbs had higher overdose rates than the city. She knew part of the reason for this was that suburban places didn't have quick access to harm reduction supplies, so many deaths happened there beyond the reach of harm reduction workers. But it was the toxicology she was most interested in. As she scrolled down the page, she noticed something very peculiar. There were not many overdose cases involving xylazine in the suburbs. Xylazine was an animal tranquilizer that didn't respond to Narcan, and it was wreaking havoc on the homeless population.

In her experience, the dope all started in one place, and then it was cut by different wholesalers as it made its way to the bottom. Somewhere along the line, it had been laced with xylazine, but it wasn't everywhere. It was focused on a certain demographic. She flipped through reports that showed xylazine at 80% in some cases. Benzos too. The suburban stuff was cut too – that was obvious – but it was cut with regular things for the sake of making money. This xylazine and benzo concoction looked as if it was being distributed for one reason: death.

What kind of dealer wants you to die? The idea is to keep you coming back – not to have you resistant to Narcan during an overdose. This doesn't make any sense economically.

She thought about the drug trafficker floating in the river. *What's your story?* She thought to herself. She looked through the data base at the victim's priors: Drug trafficking, assault, aggravated assault, unlawful confinement, impersonating an officer, and the list went on. Rob Peck was a heavy hitter. He had served time in both Joyceville and Collins Bay. She searched the police report, but it looked like a one-off. The street taking care of its own. Yet she couldn't be sure. She closed down her programs and turned off her desk light. She leaned back and looked at the ceiling. "Tomorrow is another day," she said to herself as she grabbed her jacket and headed to the elevator.

12

WHEN MIKAH GOT OFF WORK AT 10:00 P.M., SHE LOOKED DOWN AT HER phone and read a text from Charles that said, "Do you want to go for a walk on Saturday?" She stared at it for a long time and then put the phone in her pocket. She wouldn't respond tonight. It was only Wednesday.

Let him sweat a little, she thought. She just couldn't get the thought of his blue eyes out of her mind. She felt so small compared to him. She liked it. Something about him made her feel safe. She thought back to the overdose cases and wondered if they were okay. They never got to find out what happened with people unless they came back. "Professional distance" it was called. It felt more like professional torture. How could they not get up? She couldn't imagine what she would do if someone died in front of her.

She wiped it from her mind and stared out into the blackness and thought about his hair. This pandemic had made dating impossible for her. She had broken up with her high-school sweetheart before it began, and since then, she hadn't been around anyone new. She felt all those old feelings of want return to her. She couldn't shake it. She looked at the text again and then went home and fell asleep.

Her dreams were full of saves at work. She woke in the middle of the night and thought of Charles again. *What is wrong with me?* she thought as she drank a glass of water and stood beside the fridge at 3:00 a.m. She ran her hand up the side of her thigh and around to the small of her back. She took a deep breath, closed the fridge, and went to lie back down. She stared at the ceiling and imagined her future. A master's in a couple years and research after that. She felt safer behind the data than she did collecting it.

She wondered if people ever got used to her job. It was crazy: highs, lows; the tragedy; the rawness of people's emotions. She needed the next hour to settle all the images she had collected in her mind. It felt like a movie that she was watching. It didn't feel like it was happening to her at all. She fell back asleep sometime later; drifting off into places unknown to her; drifting off into places soon to come to her.

13

WHEN MIKAH GOT TO WORK THE NEXT DAY, SHE HEARD THE NEWS: TWO of the three people who overdosed in her unit had died on the way to the hospital. She sat down at the computer and absorbed the news. She wanted to know which ones had died so she could specify if it was hers. The deceased were new to everybody but Perry. He was the one who let everyone know their status. He knew the one girl who lived, and it was her mother's phone call to Perry that gave them all the scoop.

"This dope is fucked," Perry said, shaking his head as he took a sip of his coffee. The place was quiet and empty for a Thursday.

"Pretty quiet in here today," Susan said as she came out of her office. Susan was the manager. She only came out of her office when she wasn't swamped with orders or scheduling and hiring. The turnaround in a place like this was astonishing. Mikah sat up and didn't talk when Susan was on the floor. "I heard there were a half dozen overdoses yesterday besides us," Susan said.

"Any deaths?" Perry asked.

"Not that I know of besides the ones that were in here," Susan said.

Just then Tdot and K-ultra came through the door. "Fuck you, cunt. It's mine," K-ultra said as he ran to the far booth.

"I didn't want it anyway, champ," Tdot said with a laugh.

"Fuck off," K-ultra returned.

"Guess what, guys?" Tdot said interrupting the conversation entirely.

"What's up?" Susan asked.

"Yesterday, when K-ultra was collecting bottles, some guy comes out of the alley and yells, 'Fuck you, this is my turf,' so K punched him out. So now it's like his turf!" Tdot said, jumping up and down and scratching his left arm. K-ultra started to laugh.

"But that's not the funniest part because K can't remember where he was when it happened!" he said, laughing.

"So now you don't even know where your turf is," Perry said, smiling.

"Fuckin goof that guy was, over bottles. Who calls turf over fucking bottles?" K-ultra said with a laugh, shifting in his chair as he made up his shot.

Just then, Tdot started showing Kelly, who was fixing in one of the other booths, some of the stuff he had boosted. She had been their only customer so far before Tdot and K-ultra had showed up. "Check this out girl: Versace shirt, and all that," he said as he rifled through the bag. "I know where there's tons more, but I only took a few pieces. Maybe some time you should come with me. I know a spot, and I have a way in. You can grab a garbage bag full of stuff," Tdot said.

In that moment, Kelly looked up at him. She was sweating, and her eyes were half pinned from dope. She said with a big smile and a flash of her blue eyes, "I want to go on a rampage with you."

Susan looked over at the two of them and said, "Aww, they're so cute."

Mikah watched K-ultra as he started to nod in and out. "Did you guys check your dope?" Mikah asked in his direction.

"I don't buy from ghosts," K-ultra said as he opened his eyes and took a deep breath.

"Who's that?" Mikah asked.

"Ask no questions, hear no lies," K-ultra said as he pulled the rig from his vein and threw it on the table with two fingers. "Are you fixing or what moron?!" He yelled in no particular direction.

"Yeah, yeah," Tdot said, fixing the cooker between his fingers and lighting the bottom. He made two shots, one for him and one for Kelly, and fixed quickly. "See ya, later girl," he said as she rested her elbow on the side of the booth she was sitting in and closed her eyes.

Mikah watched her chest go up and down and relaxed. She remembered her training: "Breathing is what you want, no matter how shallow or sporadic." Mikah was learning to watch people nod. It was a skill. She did it constantly in the observation tank. People would nod and sleep in there all day, and if she was stationed in there, she would watch people's chests rise and fall. Some were peaceful and some twitched endlessly, but all in all, they looked peaceful. Safe even. Safe away from those streets for just a little while.

14

DAX SAT AT THE PARK LAWN CEMETERY OFF OF BLOOR STREET AND WAITED for his contact. He had been summoned. He looked over the gravestones and studied their dates and sayings. Some were religious, some descriptive, and others were poetic. His grave would read: "I took who I needed and left the rest."

Just then, he saw a large figure walking towards him. It was Charon. He was dressed in designer clothes and sunglasses, but it was him. Dax straightened himself out and stood up to shake the man's hand. "Hey, I didn't expect you," Dax said surprised.

"Well, I couldn't help myself after the other day. That was quite the kill," Charon said.

"Yeah, I wish I could have got in the tent, but I did what I had too," Dax said ashamed a little for not collecting the soul of someone so young.

"Don't worry about that. I have a man at the church who paid her fare across the river. Great work," he said reassuringly.

"Thanks," Dax said relieved. Perfection was something he strived for in his work.

Charon looked off into the distance for a moment and tilted his head back and took a deep breath. Spring was upon them, and all the smells that intimate summer were in the air. They could have been just a couple of guys taking a stroll in another life.

"I wanted to ask you something," Dax said nervously.

"What?" Charon said as he looked Dax in the eyes. Even through his sunglasses, Dax could still see how intense Charon's blue eyes were.

"Where do they go?" Dax asked.

"Oh, I can't tell you that; it would ruin the surprise," Charon said.

Dax knew Charon's work had evolved past trophy kills to be left out where everyone could see them. Charon made people disappear. So many kills, so many souls, where did he put them? Dax was intrigued and jealous. How could a man so young create something so beautiful? Dax was lost for words after that.

"Keep up the great work, and one day I might call on you," Charon said patting Dax on the shoulder.

"And I'll be waiting diligently, sir," Dax said as he watched Charon make his way past the graves and out of sight. It seemed that his shadow stayed on the graves he passed long after he had. Dax felt energized and focused after his meeting. He couldn't wait to get back out there. He relished nightfall just like he did when he first started. He felt the vibrancy of his youth ignited by the young man. "And all of hell followed with him," was all he heard as he caned his way up Bloor.

15

AMY READ THE PATHOLOGY REPORT FROM THE DEATHS AT THE SAFE INJECtion site the day before. "Dead on route." She had never seen that before coming out of a safe injection site. The toxicology report found xylazine, cannabinoids, benzo, and fentanyl. The pathology report was congruent with other recent downtown episodes of overdose.

This is doctored dope, she thought. *This dope is created to do one thing: fight Narcan reversal.* She looked through the police reports and noticed that if the date was changed on each report, they would all look the same. *'What did they create an efficiency program to make these faster?'* she asked herself. *'This is only getting worse,* she thought as she closed the file on her computer and leaned back in her chair.

She recalled a time before the pandemic when the city had 450 drug-related deaths. She had thought that was bad. Since the pandemic hit, the numbers had doubled to 850 in 2020. 2021 had already seen a record-breaking month in January with 36 deaths. This year was set to break historical numbers, and she was lost. She felt like the passenger of a Mack Truck going the wrong way on the 407. So many people could die, and there was nothing she could do about it. Her hands were tied. She packed up her things and headed home for the night. Tomorrow was another day.

16

SATURDAY WAS APPROACHING AS MIKAH LAY ON HER BED FRIDAY MORNING. It was her first day off out of four. She couldn't move. She felt as though her life was slipping away from her. She ate, slept, and cried. She repeated this motion continuously. She would watch Netflix and scroll through things on her phone, and then she would remember the faces of the dead, and she would cry. She went into the kitchen and ate. She looked out the window at the cherry blossom buds and felt elated, but then that would fade back into black. She wanted to crawl under the covers and sleep. She didn't want to go back, but she knew she had to. She didn't know where she would get the strength, but she knew she would.

She looked at his recent text: "Are you still free Saturday?"

She responded, "Maybe in the afternoon," to which he said, "Perfect."

She slumped back down beneath the covers and fell asleep. "Tomorrow will be better," she said to herself as she slipped away down into the depths of her psyche. She would find the strength somewhere down there. Somewhere down there her strength was waiting to be found.

17

"CAN WE MEET AT QUEEN'S PARK AROUND 1?"

She had been staring at the text periodically since 7:30 a.m. when she had woken up. Mikah lay in her bed running down the list of reasons she didn't need a boyfriend: time consuming, demanding, immature. This was followed by a litany of unwanted pros: he's cute; I haven't been out on a date in a year; maybe it will be fun. This was followed by: What am I going wear? and I can finally wear that shirt.

"Okay," was all she said.

He was sitting on a bench when she first saw him. He looked off into the distance, probably expecting her to come from another way. She studied him for a moment and almost stopped. His broad shoulders seemed to hold him in place like a soldier. His face was sculpted perfectly, and the way the sun hit it gave his eyes a twinkle of diamond. In that moment, he looked over at her, and her knees gave way a bit. She put one hand out to steady her walk. She felt exposed to him all of a sudden, and she quickly pulled everything back inside her again and gave him the business end of her persona.

"Good afternoon, Charles. Have you been here long?" she said as if she were conducting an interview.

"Not long at all," he said as he stood to meet her. Neither person was sure of an embrace, so that is probably why it never took place. Neither wore a mask, which was comforting on some level. "I thought you would feel most comfortable in your old stomping grounds," he said reassuringly.

"Yeah, it does bring back memories, feels like years ago that I went here," she said as she reached back for a memory from a simpler time.

"It's been a crazy year," Charlie said as he looked towards the ground, not knowing what to say.

"What do you do? Besides asking women out at the Tim Hortons?" she said to sass him a bit and see how he handled it.

"I work at a funeral home," he said.

She wasn't expecting that at all. She didn't know what to say next, but he seemed to just take over the conversation after that. He explained that after he got his degree in History from the University of Toronto, he worked at a bunch of different jobs to give himself a break. Mikah understood that. He said that he had a friend whose parents ran a funeral home, and they needed some help during the high season (winter was the busiest season because of flu deaths).

"You must be booming now," she said.

He looked her in the eye with those blue eyes of his and said, "You have no idea," which sent chills down her spine. He explained that he started working there to help out, and now he was on full time, filling in and helping with the business.

She didn't know what to say, so she didn't say anything. She remembered the old adage: "A man will tell you who he is, if you just listen." So that's what she did. Just like in school, she would study his inferences to things and make deductions. He was a Type A personality, goal oriented, risk taking, and a born leader. She studied his movements and the way he would look off into the distance.

He reminded her of those rugby players in New Zealand, the All Blacks. They were fierce competitors, but when they did the ceremonial Haka dance, they revealed a part of their personalities that was both soft and terrifying at the same time. She didn't like to feel scared of him but knew it was important. She was instantly woken from her musings about him by his question, "Are you afraid of ghosts?"

She was taken aback. "Why?" she asked.

"I have a surprise for you," he said.

"What?" she asked as she looked at his face, searching it for an answer.

He pointed up in the sky at the tallest building in sight and said, "Have you ever been up there?"

Mikah looked up and recognized the Whitney Block Tower. "Nobody has been in there since the 60s. it's abandoned," she said.

"I didn't ask you if anybody was allowed in; I asked you if you were afraid of ghosts," he followed playfully.

"No," Mikah said finally after a moment.

"Would you like to see it?" he said motioning her to come with him.

"I've always wanted to go in there. I've been staring at that tower for years," she said as she followed him across the street and down some steps outside the government buildings.

"C'mon," he said as he opened a door with a key.

She stopped for a moment and resisted. How much did she really know about him? She stood there and felt a tug from inside her. She was drawn to him. He was mysterious and exciting; she wasn't used to that. "Where does this go?" she asked.

"The tunnel," he said as he put his hand on her back and led her into a dark hallway that had light bulbs lining the top edge.

She felt like she was in a tomb all of a sudden, and she got scared. "How did you do this?" she asked, following him down the hallway.

"I know people," he said with a laugh. "Now, do you want to take the stairs or use the hand-cranked elevator?" he asked with a laugh.

"Let's take the stairs," she said. A hand-cranked elevator sounded like a death trap to her. She started to follow him up the stairs. With every flight, she began sweating a bit more. It seemed to get hotter as they climbed.

"There is no ventilation in the building unless you open the windows, so it will get a little hot," he said as his voice echoed in the staircase. When they got halfway up, he opened a door and led her into a huge empty space with twenty-foot ceilings and dust covering everything like a layer of snow. She looked out the windows and could see the whole city.

He led her into a room with cages, and she got scared for a second. "This is where they used to have a veterinarian clinic in the 60s. You can see the cages are still here," he said.

She marveled at the dust-filled glass and wiped some off of one of the cases to see what was inside. In that moment she sneezed heavily.

"Oh, don't worry. They didn't have COVID back then," he said with a laugh. They looked out the window for a moment, and then he turned to her and asked, "Are you ready to go the rest of the way?"

She looked back at him intrigued by his energy and nodded. As she climbed, it continued to get hotter and hotter.

"Some say that they used to pack ice at the top of the tower and use the downflow to cool the building," he said as he climbed flight after flight effortlessly.

At one point, Mikah yelled up to him, "Slow down, I have little legs!" With this, he steadied his pace and remembered he was on a date, not a mission.

When they reached the top, Mikah was out of breath and out of shape. He stared back at her with triumph on his face from the completion of the long, sixteen-story ascent. She walked away from his gaze to catch her breath, and he looked out into the distance. The view was beautiful; she couldn't deny that. Spring was laying its beauty all over the city, the cherry blossoms everywhere she looked. She caught her breath finally, and then went and found him. He was sitting with one foot out the window on the window ledge.

Mikah absorbed the cold spring air as it enveloped her when she walked towards him. She sneezed again. He laughed. "This old building is hella dusty," he said. She wiped her nose with her sleeve and stood there looking out. She thought how magnificent this all was, but then she questioned it.

"Who do you know that let you come in an abandoned ghost tower of a provincial government building?" she said skeptically.

"When my father died, one of his friends on the police force brought me up here to cheer me up," Charles said, staring off into the distance.

The bottom of Mikah's stomach nearly fell out. "I'm sorry," she said quickly, feeling very isolated and embarrassed all of a sudden.

"It's okay. I've never told anybody because I've never brought anyone up here," he said reassuringly.

She looked back at him, and suddenly, she had lots of questions for him that she didn't know how to ask. She was entranced by the thought of him. She stepped towards him, and it felt like she was being pulled. He stood up and turned to look out the window, and she came and stood beside him. She wanted to see where he was looking, so she kept turning to him to see where his gaze fell. She felt him slide his hand into hers and neither of them looked at each other.

"How long have you been coming here?" she asked, finally breaking the silence.

"Twelve years. Come and look out the window at the statues. One is a doctor and a child, and the other is a businessman," he said, changing the subject. Mikah looked out the window at the statues with Charles standing behind her.

"Oh wow, we are so high up," Mikah said taking in the height.

"Yeah, it's quite the drop," Charles said, watching Mikah quietly from a distance. When Mikah was finished studying the statues, she swung her leg in from the ledge. She stood up and dusted off her legs and sneezed again. They both laughed and then he sneezed too. "If we were sneezing like this down there, people would be freaking out," Charles said with a laugh.

"They would probably call the cops," Mikah laughed. "Nobody at my work wears a mask though; that population seems to be indifferent to it," Mikah said.

"I bet," Charles said coldly.

She quickly changed the tone by walking to the other end of the room and studying the view of the city from that side. "It's so beautiful," she said as he walked towards her, taking in what she was seeing.

"It is," he said staring right at her.

Chills ran up and down Mikah's body as she ran her hand down her thigh to meet them. She looked back at him, and he closed the distance between them, making Mikah look up at him. She closed her eyes as he brought his face close to hers, and she felt his soft lips touch hers. She was filled with exhilaration. She put her hand on his back and felt the solidness of his being. He ran his hands up her back, pulling her up and close to him, kissing her, and then he, let go completely. Mikah's heels slowly descended back onto the ground as he let her go. They both stared at each other and then they both looked away.

The rest of the afternoon was filled with putting the distance back between them. She followed him back down the tower and then through the tunnel. They never really spoke. He walked her back across the street and through the park. Spring began to surround them everywhere they looked; green buds were popping up everywhere. They reached the place where they had started, and it felt like they were seeing it for the first time.

Returning back to her apartment, Mikah felt as if she had sailed home. She had forgotten about everything. *What a difference one afternoon makes,* she thought. She was no longer weighed down by the dark aspect that she had been carrying around. It had been replaced by something new; something she had been waiting for but could not name. It took her a long time to come back to her baseline.

She found herself looking at her phone constantly until it came: "I had a great time today."

She took a deep breath, fell onto her bed, screamed in excitement into her pillow, and cried. As tears streamed down her face, she felt reborn to herself and to the world.

"I did too," was all she replied. She fell asleep that night with ease. Her strength had returned. She had borrowed it from him.

18

ON MONDAY MORNING, MIKAH SAT AT HER DESK INSIDE THE SITE, SIPPING her coffee and watching the first participants shuffle in. She studied them as they walked by. None of them would wear a mask voluntarily, regardless of the lockdown procedures that were everywhere. It agitated her that this population, as vulnerable as it was, would forgo safety measures so flagrantly. She took a sip of her coffee, ground her teeth, and turned to Perry, asking, "Why don't they wear masks? I see them everywhere without one."

She heard one of the men on the far end say, "I wear a mask, whenever I need to boost shit from a store. They won't let me in without one," he laughed. She shook her head in disbelief.

Perry turned to her and said, "Maybe they are just returning the favor." He looked tired.

"For what?" she asked, and it felt as if the whole room went quiet to hear him respond.

"Where were you last year when this all began?" Perry asked.

"In school," she responded.

"So, you were at home then?" he said, finishing her sentence. "Last year, when this began, you could only find COVID in an airport. They shut down all our essential services to prepare for it – as if these people here had some home to go to. They shut down homeless shelters and forced these people into the encampments. They shut down our facilities. They wouldn't let these people shower and go to the bathroom inside any buildings. They shut down bottle depots and eradicated the use of cash. It was a direct assault on their way of life.

"I know at least thirty people in this population that have died of overdoses. Friends, coworkers, and community leaders. Nothing was done for these people. They were hit the hardest. They are supposed to be a vulnerable population, not an invisible one. The overdose rate has doubled since the pandemic began, and so has the rate for drug-related deaths. The fear and pure terror that was foisted upon them out here was beyond compare.

"So, you ask me why they don't wear masks? Would you wear a mask if that was the life you had to endure since the inception of them? They don't see it as a health precaution. They see it as a direct act of genocide against them. Do you know how many people are missing? I know of dozens. Who shuts down emergency services during an emergency?" Perry said finally catching his breath. The whole room started clapping and hollering. It startled Mikah. She had never seen them as a group before, just as individuals using drugs. She hadn't seen them as a community that was interwoven like tapestry. If you hurt one, you hurt them all.

19

AMY SAT IN HER OFFICE MONDAY MORNING SORTING THROUGH THE weekend reports. Another mid-level drug pusher had been found floating in the water under the Queen Street viaduct. It was the same as the last one: overdosed with coins lodged in his throat. No witnesses. She thought to herself about what Ahmed had said about Charontas and the River Styx. She read the pathology report: The body had been washed clean of evidence because of the water. Amy also read the police report, but it seemed routine. No leads, and the victim had a lengthy prison record and many enemies. Another bag-and-tag job. Plus, there had been six overdose deaths over the weekend. All but one was in the suburbs, with no trace of xylazine in the pathology reports. "This city," she said to herself. "We are going to have another record-setting month."

20

DAX CANED HIS WAY DOWN QUEEN STREET EAST HOPING TO GET LUCKY. The sun set on the horizon as he surveyed the street corners that were scraped clean from the restrictions. "Not a lot of luck tonight," he said to himself as he shook off the cold and lit a cigarette. *Maybe I'll swing back up to Alexander Park,* he thought. He had to watch how frequently he cased each neighborhood. He didn't want to develop a pattern. The one thing the legion was strict on was spreading the work around, so it didn't look strategic. Things had to look random. Never take souls from the same place. Men would travel to all the boroughs because of this: Scarborough, Brampton, East York, North York, and Etobicoke.

Dax sat for a moment and took it all in. *With the amount of souls, we are taking, we might be able to end homelessness.* He laughed to himself as he flicked his cigarette into the last trail of smoke he exhaled. He continued to scan the corners as he caned his way up the street. So many were hiding inside; so many were blind to all that was really going on. He had to thank Lady Pandemic for creating the perfect conditions for his vocation. Never since he had begun taking souls had it been this easy. People rarely thought about his victims to begin with, but now… now he could pillage with impunity.

He smiled as he saw a street walker coming towards him. She looked tired.

"You lookin?" she said looking at his cane.

"Where could we go?" Dax said in a low, innocent voice.

"I know a place," she said.

"Down to trade?" he asked.

"Perfect honey, just follow me," she replied, leading the way.

Dax looked up at the sky and thought, *Luck be my lady tonight.*

21

MIKAH WAS STARTING TO SEE THROUGH NEW EYES SINCE MONDAY. SHE watched this disheveled population interact in a different way than ever before. She started to see beyond the screaming and yelling, the crying and the wailing, the using and the nodding, and the constant movement. She started to see a host of coping mechanisms to trauma. It was one thing to read about it in a book or see some socialite complain that they were suffering from it on social media.

This was different. These people had all the identifiers of it but didn't know it. They weren't blaming it on anything. They were acting it out. They used their traumatic shortcuts as a way to circumvent any and all stress. They ticked, they talked, they scratched, they kicked, they screamed, they leaned, and they bent. They got high, they got low, and they would repeat the cycle day in and day out. Mikah got to know the names of the participants, their drug of choice, and their traumas. She tried her best to serve their needs and stay out of their way.

"This isn't recovery," Perry would say. "No codependent bleeding hearts here." He said that any time anyone talked to a participant about getting "clean". Perry would say that the second you talk about that here without them bringing it up, you were driving a wedge between you. "Recovery doesn't need to be promoted; they all know what it is. The minute you talk about their recovery, you'll lose them. They are all ears to listen to stories about other people, but never what they should be doing.

"Your job is to keep them alive and help them get high. If they need something from you, they will let you know. Don't try and save anyone, or you'll be the one who needs saving. You will drown in a codependent cauldron like they do in those twelve-step groups."

Mikah could see the trauma on her coworkers too. Nervous ticks, over-reactions, drama – it was all there, in plain sight, if you had the eyes to see it.

Mikah looked over at Tdot Tuesday afternoon and asked him about his handle.

"It's Tdot because I am this city, born and bred, and on the street since day one; this city is my lady. We've been through it all," he said to her as he turned his hat sideways and stuck his tongue out at himself in the mirror in his booth.

"You should tell your lady to find us some dope!" K-ultra yelled from the other side of the room.

"Why? So, I can Narcan you again like last night, you fuckin lush?" Tdot said.

"Yeah, yeah, one night," K-ultra returned to which Tdot looked at Mikah and mouthed the words "every night" with a smile.

"I ain't like you guys here though. I wait till his lips turn blue. I'm not looking for stats," he laughed and Mikah laughed too.

These guys blew her away. K-ultra overdosed all the time, apparently. These two dudes just rolled around the city getting into adventures. They were on the edge of life and death, every day. They weren't afraid to die; they seemed to thrive on the edge. They all did. Death was staring them all in the face every moment, but they seemed to be warm to it or at least to tolerate it as a constant companion.

When Mikah left her work, she started to look at the people in the street with skepticism. *What are these people so afraid of?* she thought. *Especially the old people who seem to be clinging to the last drop of life they have in them. They are afraid to let go.*

She borrowed courage from her participants and walked home with her head held high. She wasn't afraid to die; she borrowed that from them. She was free of the fear that gripped her city. She walked with confidence. The unknown would be kind to her because she did not fear it.

22

IN THE DAYS FOLLOWING CHARLES' FATHER'S DEATH, HE FOUND HIMSELF trying to be strong for his mother. He sat across from her, in Pinkett's Funeral Home on Dundas Street, holding her while she cried continuously. He looked around the place for something to focus on that would calm his grief. He found an angel inside one of the paintings on the wall and focused on it while he felt his mother slipping away. At seventeen, Charles had never known anyone who had died before. It seemed like it was more something you saw on TV than reality.

The funeral home was just a big house with the business on the first floor and the residence upstairs. He spent a lot of time there that week. He met the Pinkett's son Jonathon, who was Charles' age, and the two of them played video games upstairs before and after the funeral service. A police funeral was no small occasion. There was a parade of first responders from around the province and numerous news crews; the pomp and pageantry overwhelmed Charles and his mother.

The news reported that a junkie had killed his father and suggested that if the man had been properly taken care of in the community by hospitals and police, this wouldn't have happened. Charles could still hear his mother screaming out of the car window at the journalists as she drove out of her driveway: "You think this happened because of us!"

After the funeral, when all the well-wishers had left, his mother wouldn't come out of her room for weeks. Charles would go in there at night and sleep in her bed with her. Her side felt cold to him, and her face was losing colour. He started to stay home from school to look after her. There wasn't anything he could do.

One night she urged him to go and play video games with Jonathon. She promised she would be fine. The last time Charles saw his mother was when he arrived home that night and found her dead in the bathtub. She had cut her wrists. Charles reached into the cold water and pulled her close, but she was gone. He sat soaking wet in the corner of the bathroom and refused to move. The police brought in a social worker, and they talked Charles out of the bathroom and into his own room. He was told to pack a bag.

He spent a lot of time with Jonathon at the Pinketts' house after that. His mother's funeral was also held at Pinkett's, and Charles had to undergo the whole nightmare again, but alone this time. He stared at the angel on the wall, and it seemed to place a halo over the noise and commotion that surrounded him. His parents were buried together, side by side, in Mount Hope Cemetery. When Cynthia and Robert Pinkett heard that Charles would be placed in foster care, they decided to adopt him. Charles was thrilled to be able to stay around Jonathon. They had become such good friends through the tragedy that Charles held on to their friendship tightly.

Charles assumed a new life there with the Pinketts. Cynthia ran the day-to-day operations. Robert took care of all the basement activities of preparing bodies and cremating the dead. The house always smelt of fresh flowers and formaldehyde. Cynthia had inherited the property from her parents, who had moved to Florida. They had three bedrooms upstairs equipped with office space, a kitchen and a huge living room, where Jonathon and Charles played Xbox on a sixty four-inch screen television. Cynthia was either in her office or the kitchen while Robert transported bodies around town or worked in the basement.

They were very happy to take in Charles. Jonathon needed a real friend. He was a loner at school and spent much of his time gaming at home. Cynthia would often say that: "God had found him a friend." There was no need for Jonathon to explain his life to Charles like he had to with the other kids at school. Charles was very grateful to the Pinkett's for everything, and he saw the value in their business. The two young men went to school together and then played video games until their eyes were bloodshot and they fell asleep in the living room. The two young men were inseparable.

Charles would stay upstairs during the funerals at first, but after watching Jonathon perform all the duties that were required of him, Charles started to help. They would wash the cars and set up chairs. They would make food and pick up flower arrangements. Charles had never moved far away from the feeling that consumed him when his parents died, so now he learned to live close to it. He found a comfort in other people's grief. He knew he wasn't alone.

It wasn't until he was eighteen that Charles started to drive around with Robert and collect the "completed" people from rest homes, hospitals, and even the morgue. Charles was a regular "old hand" in the business, Robert would say. He was curious and had an understanding that came only to few. Jonathon got into MIT in Cambridge, Massachusetts, so he would be moving down there. Charles decided to pursue a history degree at the University of Toronto. He would help the Pinkett's with the business in Jonathon's absence. Charles carried on this way for years, taking classes that centered around medieval history and mythology while he worked for the Pinkett's at the funeral home.

Charles was all but over his parents' death when he walked home after school one night down Dundas Street. He was changing songs on his phone and didn't hear the man come up behind him. He couldn't hear the voice clearly over his ear buds, but he felt the knife against his neck. His ear buds were ripped from his ears, and his phone fell to the ground as a voice yelled in his ear, "Give me everything, or you die right here, right now." Charles' heart pounded in his throat, and his breathing was panicked.

Slowly his breathing slowed, and his pulse steadied. He reached back to pull out his wallet when he saw the knife move away from his throat. He quickly turned and grabbed it. He forced the man back towards a wall, and they both fell to the ground as they toppled over some garbage cans and trash bags. Charles plunged the knife into the man's throat and blood started spilling out of his neck. Charles got up quickly and watched as the man on the ground grabbed his throat with both hands and choked on his own blood. Charles found his phone on the ground and looked at it for a moment. He then looked back at the man who had terror in his eyes. The man rolled back and forth, losing energy as he did it. Charles watched the man take his last breath, and then he quickly grabbed the knife off the ground and wiped it off.

He looked around for witnesses, but it was a dark and dreary night on Dundas, and nobody was around. Charles kicked a few garbage bags in the body's direction to hide it from sight and then turned and walked away. He was terrified all the way home. Every siren he heard he thought was coming for him. When he arrived home, he went directly to the crematorium in the basement and incinerated the clothes he had on. He took a shower in the basement with his heart pounding and went up to bed. The house was quiet. The Pinkett's had long been in bed, and they never woke when Charles came home late.

Charles lay in bed, with his heart pounding for hours. The thought of his father came back to him in waves. He felt closer to him somehow. He could feel the warmth and love he had been missing come rushing through his veins. He didn't want to go to sleep. He knew when he woke, he would have to return to the life that comes after that feeling: a life of compliance and structure; a life devoid of passion and love. He lay there in the dark, and he felt free from his grief and his sad history. He was released from the land of the dead. He had come across the river to collect a soul that didn't deserve to live.

Charles thought back to the angel on the wall downstairs. Robert had explained to him that St. Michael had cast Satan out of paradise and that is what was depicted there in the painting in the living room. "You have to shine your light on the world," he would say, "to keep the bad spirits from the door."

Charles finally fell asleep in the twilight of his new existence. When he woke, the news hadn't reported the death yet, and he was stressed all day. He passed by the spot where he had left the body, and there was nothing there. He wondered if he had dreamt it. The next day, he saw it in the newspaper on page 38. The first time you kill someone is terrifying, but the first time you get away with it, that's transcendence. Charles could feel his purpose in the world all around him. He watched the junkies and hookers as he walked the streets: they weren't human to him. They represented all that was wrong with the city. Bleeding hearts defended them, but when the lights went out and all the caring professions were snug in their beds, these parasites lurked in the shadows and destroyed the city. They were already dead to him; they just didn't know it yet.

23

MIKAH'S HEAD SNAPPED AWAY FROM HER COMPUTER SCREEN TO MEET THE loud banging that came from the other side of the door. "If you guys are done in your booth, please move along into the next room. We have a big lineup of people outside," Mikah said as her heart pounded in her ear.

"Hurry up, you fuckin goofs!" she could hear Tdot yelling from the other side of the door.

There was only a small number of booths in the facility, and often the need exceeded the supply. Then there would be screaming matches in the waiting room and very slow movement inside. The atmosphere was tense. Mikah felt her neck muscles tighten to meet the stress. She would often look over at Perry, but he wouldn't acknowledge her plight.

"I'll go," Kevin said in a low tone gathering the things in his booth.

"Thank you, Kevin," Mikah said.

She liked the older gentlemen who came in to use. They seemed a lot more graceful than most. They did what they had to do, helped others, and then left without a fuss. It was refreshing. Just as Mikah wiped out Kevin's booth, the doors opened, and a familiar voice came yelling into the facility.

"What the fuck is going on in here?!" Tdot screamed as he shuffled his feet to the open booth. "Fucking dinosaurs in here," he yelled, flashing his crooked teeth and growling like a dog at everyone.

"Shut the fuck up," Rachel yelled over to him. She had been doing her makeup in the mirror for twenty minutes now.

"Fuck you, whore. Smash and get out!" he yelled as he dumped out his gear on the table and went to work. The room fell silent after that, and Tdot fixed and calmed down.

"The drugs babysit them," Mikah could hear Perry's voice in her head. She looked over at him and he was staring at the back of Tdot's head. Perry stood up and watched Tdot nod in and out. After a few minutes, Perry picked up the paper and started reading it again. Mikah knew that the window for overdose was small. If the person didn't go down in the first five minutes, they wouldn't go down at all. Tdot didn't make a sound after that until K-ultra came through the door.

"Do you get it?" K-ultra yelled, waking Tdot out of his trance.

"Here," he said in a muffled voice.

K-ultra followed the same routine. He yelled at a few people, pointed at one in the other room, and then got down to business. Perry did the same with K-ultra. He stood, watched, and then sat back down and read the paper.

"I'm surprised that these two are still alive," Mikah said to Perry under her breath.

"Yeah, they have been doing this a long time," Perry said in return. "It's not always up to you," Perry added nonchalantly.

"What do you mean?" Mikah asked.

"Well, I remember back when I was using, I tried to die many times, but it never worked. I always woke up. Didn't matter how much I used; I always woke up. I see that a lot around here too. Some people drop and die immediately, while others stay on; there's no rhyme or reason to it," he said.

"To what?" Mikah asked.

"To death – death does not think," Perry answered.

Mikah sat back and took it in. She had never thought about death like that before. Perry put his paper down and looked across the booths and said, "It's a funny thing. The people I didn't think would make it do, while the ones I thought would, don't. Recovery was the same. Anybody who came in that I thought would make it never did, and the people I thought wouldn't, did."

Perry rubbed his sides and walked around slowly. "This job is destroying my back," he said with a moan. "Too much sitting around. At least in construction you are moving around. You are always in pain there too, but it's a different pain."

Mikah went out for lunch after that. She sat on the steps across the street and looked at her building. She pulled her phone out and read the text from Charles again. "Do you want to go out again this weekend?" She hadn't answered it yet from yesterday. She looked up at the sky and squinted at the sun. It felt like she worked at a casino; all that artificial light for twelve hours a day. When she walked out and looked at the sun, she felt like those men who played poker all night.

"Okay," was all she replied. She liked having something to look forward to away from this place. She finished her sandwich and drank her coffee, stood up, stretched and walked back in to work. When she got inside, it was quiet. She exhaled a deep breath. Ever since she had come in to the three overdoses, she imagined it happening everywhere she went. She even imagined it when she walked into the Tim Hortons. She sat down and watched Tdot shake and twitch with his face up against the side of his booth.

"Movement and breath are good signs," she heard Perry's voice say inside her head.

24

Amy woke to a blanket text message sent out by the provincial government about a province-wide, April 1st "stay at home order". A new lockdown order was in place for four weeks. Restaurants, travel, and purchase restrictions abounded in news reports across the province. Walmart had roped off the sections of clothing and other novelty items; only essentials were being sold. Amy looked at the pictures of her teenage daughters and wondered how much fun they were all about to have being stuck at home together. *The girls can sleep in, so at least they'll be happy about that,* she thought. Working from home had its perks, such as being able to work in your pajamas and not having to pay for lunch and coffee.

She turned on her computer and responded to an email she had received from Detective Mason from homicide. She decided to give him a call after she had her first coffee, half empty and in hand. She sat down at the kitchen table and looked out the window as the phone rang. "Hello, Homicide," the voice on the other end answered.

How cheery, she thought.

"Hello, good morning. This is Amy Winter from the Coroner's Office. Is this Detective Mason?"

"Yes. Good morning," he said clearing his throat momentarily.

"Well, I won't waste any time getting to it. I want to ask you about the two bodies in the river. What can you tell me that I can't read in the report?" she finished.

"Well, to start with, both of the men were criminal informants. We were sorry to lose them both so quickly," he said in a low tone.

"Interesting. So, you can connect them up to something else?" she asked, quickly trying to build momentum.

"Both men were dealing for a crew called the "Legion", but we don't really know much about them. The CI's rarely knew who they were working for. There was a lot of night drops and burners being used for communication. The one thing they did know is that these people were making everything themselves."

Amy nodded her head in agreement and said, "Yeah, that would make sense. These murders fit a pattern downtown that you can't really find in the suburbs. The volume of it doesn't make sense economically," she responded.

"That's the strangest part about this case. We have no idea who these guys are," Mason said finally.

"How long was this going on?" Amy asked.

"At least a year," Mason said.

"What!? You've known about this for a year?" she gasped.

"Yes, but none of it added up. The dope and the pandemic – it was all so strange. We thought the guys were lying to us, and that we couldn't trust them. They never got anybody on tape, text, or anything. It seemed too fantastic, so we just waited." Mason said, finally exhaling.

"Now they're both dead in a short span of time. What does that mean to you?" Amy asked.

"That they weren't needed anymore, and they got killed for it," Mason answered.

"Well, the supply hasn't dried up. I still have people dying every day from this stuff, so the buck didn't stop with them," Amy said finally after a pause.

"We were taken back by it as well, especially the second guy," he said.

"Why?" she asked quickly.

"He told us he was about to receive thirty kilos, and then we found him in the river."

"What? How come this isn't in the report?" Amy accused.

"It's still part of an ongoing investigation. We will catch you up when we have something," he returned.

"Thirty kilos of that dope? That will kill a lot of people," she said thinking out loud.

"We think that was the point. The Legion, or whatever, knows that the pandemic is coming to an end, so it is trying to get as many people as it can." Mason answered.

"A year?" Amy asked again, just so she could hear it again.

"A year," Mason returned.

"And you will let me know about any and all further developments?" she commanded.

"Yes, when we know, you'll know."

Amy typed up a drug advisory notice and sent it to the mayor and health authority right after she hung up the phone. This was big. She was right; this was deliberate. Her head spun in a million directions as she watched both of her daughters emerge from their rooms expecting breakfast because she was home.

25

DAX LEFT HIS BASEMENT APARTMENT AND MET WITH HIS REGULAR contact at the Rosedale Ravine Park.

"Did you see the announcement this morning about the shutdown?" he was asked.

"Kinda hard to miss," Dax said lighting a cigarette.

"This is it," was all Dax heard after that.

Dax and everyone in the Legion knew that with the vaccine being administered everywhere, the conditions that they had exploited for so long would soon be out of reach. The plan was an execution of what was called the "orange order". The decree was not new. It is well known to every native population on the planet. The imperial powers had many ways of executing the order. In the early days, it was blankets of smallpox, residential schools, and alcohol.

With the Legion, it was the xylazine dream: Twice as potent when mixed with benzos and fentanyl and Narcan resistant. It was a harm-reduction proof death scrum. The dope would be sold at rock-bottom prices all over the city, and during the pandemonium of overdose calls, the Legion would take the rest by force. Every tent, street corner, and alley would be assaulted. No prisoners and no mercy. They would end homelessness for good and all.

26

MIKAH: *CAN I ASK A FAVOR?*

    Charles: *Of course*

    Mikah: *I know this might sound weird, but can I see where you work?*

    Charles: *Okay. Meet me at Pinkett's funeral home on Dundas Street East on Saturday at 1 p.m.*

    Mikah: *Thank you.*

    Mikah was drawn to Charles because he resided at a level of society that appealed to her; a part of society she didn't realize held the greatest amount of healing for her – the death industry. She was surrounded by death and scared of it all day. At any moment, someone could drop in her unit and then they were rolling the dice until the person took their first breath. She was drawn to his confidence. She knew he held the answers for her somehow; she just didn't know how to ask the question. She felt her way to him. He had appeared in her life at just the right moment. She had met him immediately before the trauma started over the deaths in her unit. She felt like she was haunted and then she met this guy; his parents were dead, and he was happy working in a funeral home. She wanted to be in his world. She felt safe at the very thought of being near him.

    Charles was sitting on the front steps holding a mask in his hand when Mikah arrived on Saturday. "You're in luck. We don't have any COVID bodies at the moment, so we can just wear normal clothes and masks; otherwise, we would have to suit up," Charles said cheerfully as he led Mikah around back.

She followed Charles down the back stairs and through a set of double doors. "This elevator is where the body comes down. From there, we take the body into the mortuary to prepare it for embalming. We call it the sanctuary," he said, waving his arm to present a large room with a hospital bed in the middle and shelves full of plastic bottles to each side. A chair was set against the far wall, with a stereo positioned on a shelf above it. The color of the room was light blue.

Mikah felt calm and exhaled as she took the room in. She closed her eyes for a second, and when she opened them, she looked over and he was staring at her. A chill ran down her spine.

"Are you okay?" Charles asked her, putting his hand on her arm.

"Yes, it's just been a hard week," Mikah said, looking back at him and watching him relax with her comment.

He walked her into the next room. "This is the crematorium. It has four latched doors, which lead to the cremation chambers." He studied her with his eyes as she stepped forward and touched one of the handles. "This is where it all happens," Charles said finally.

"I want to say, 'Cool.' Can I say that?" she asked

"I always thought so," Charles said with a smile.

"Can I ask you how you came to work here, Charles?" she asked as he led her into a break room area with lockers and a table and chairs.

"Well, after my parents died, I had spent so much time here that the people who run it decided to adopt me, believe it or not," Charles said.

"Seriously?" Mikah asked.

"Yeah, I spent so much time playing Xbox with their son Jonathon that they asked me to stay," Charles replied.

"Can I ask what happened to your parents?" Mikah took a deep breath.

"Well, you remember that my dad was a cop, right?" Charles asked intently.

"Yes," Mikah said.

"One day he responded to a call at High Park and was killed by a junkie. My mother succumbed to grief and died shortly after that," he said calmly. She didn't know what to say next.

"So, I ended up here. Now I work for the Pinkett's," he finished.

"I'm so sorry, Charles," Mikah said quickly.

"Thank you," he returned. "I would take you upstairs, but it is full of embalmed bodies waiting to be buried. Funeral services are backed up as you could imagine with the pandemic – and now the lockdown," he said changing the subject.

"Do you have a bedroom?" Mikah said boldly. She wanted to hold him, and she knew they couldn't touch in this space.

"Yeah," was all he said as he led her up the stairs and down a hall, past two bedrooms and a living room to a door. The door opened, and he went in, sat on his bed, took his mask off. and lay down. She took hers off too, and her shoes, and lay with him there. The two lay there for hours without really speaking. She was absorbed into his body so warmly that she forgot where she was.

By the time they started having sex, she didn't know who had initiated it, but she was glad it was happening. She had only been with one person before Charles and found the differences tantalizing. As they lay in the afterglow, Charles said, "Well, I guess you're in my bubble."

"I am," Mikah said, burying her head in his shoulder.

He cleared her black hair from her eyes and kissed her face as he held her tight. She had forgotten about her work and the world as a whole. All she knew was that she never wanted to leave.

27

MONDAY MORNING CAME TOO SOON, AND MIKAH FELT LIKE SHE HAD walked out of her place into a different world. Everywhere she went, everything was closed. She wasn't even sure the bus was going to come. She had got the text sometime after she left Charles' place. Province-wide lockdown for four weeks. She had quickly texted Perry to ask if she still had to come to work, and he answered, "Thank God, we do."

When she arrived at work, the booths had been spaced out, but not closed, and observation was limited to three people. She settled into her chair and pulled up the shift reports from the weekend. They had six overdoses since she had left, but no fatalities. "You guys had some action this weekend, I see," Mikah said probing for a story.

"Yeah, I was on. It took a mountain to get one guy on his feet. The benzo effect is strong in some of this dope; not as bad as X though," Susan said.

"What's X?" Mikah asked.

"Xylazine is an animal tranquilizer. It's okay by itself in small doses but that isn't what we are seeing, it's 80% and if you mix it with fentanyl, it can be lethal because the Narcan won't counteract it," Perry answered.

"Holy shit," Mikah said. "Is that what happened with the people from the other day?"

"We think so, and apparently there is a lot more of it coming," Susan said as she slid a piece of paper over to Mikah.

"What's this?" she asked.

"The new dope advisory," Susan answered and walked back into her office. Mikah read down the list.

> Don't use alone.
> Stagger your use with a friend, so someone can respond.
> Check drugs
> Carry Naloxone.
> Do a tester before you do a regular hit.

Mikah read down the list and cringed. "Expect it to get hot around here. The province shut down two safe injection sites yesterday. We are sure to see those people and an increase ourselves because of the panic," Perry said.

"At least they didn't shut us down," Mikah said in high spirits.

"Not this time. Last year in March, they shut our doors for a month. An emergency service. An essential service. They shut our doors for safety reasons. Seven people die a week on average if we close. If you add the hysteria of a pandemic on top of that, those numbers go through the roof. How can people dying be safe? This makes no sense," Perry said, obviously pissed off.

He took a couple of deep breaths and went into it. "Do you remember the grocery stores last year? Aisles cleaned out; lineups everywhere for miles. Imagine if they had closed down the grocery store completely. Think of the pandemonium and riots that would cause. This place here is a symbol. Nobody understands that. When this place closed its doors, it was the closing of a symbol between life and death for these people. Our people aren't allowed in the grocery store at the best of times. Shutting our doors is like closing a grocery store, clinic, psychiatrist, social services, and shelter all at the same time. What we represent to these people matters. We are a beacon of hope in a very dark place. Just because someone gets COVID upstairs doesn't give them the right to kill twenty-eight of our people. It's either essential or its not," Perry said taking a drink of his coffee.

The room erupted in cheers and clapping.

"Okay, settle down," Perry said to them.

"You should run for mayor!" Tdot said from his side of the room.

"Who would help us then, moron?" K-ultra yelled from his side.

"Calm down, folks, I'm not going anywhere. I am where I belong," Perry said. "Okay everybody, if you are done with your smash move along. We got a lot of people on the list," Perry finished with a smile.

Mikah put the advisory back on the desk and sat back in her chair, absorbing what she had just learned. She thought about what she was doing last year during the lockdown and felt guilty. She had just sat around and complained about being bored to anyone who would listen. She didn't know there were people dying in the streets alone with nowhere to go. She realized that about her job. She did her job so other people didn't have to know what was happening. The job was institutionalizing drug use in the same way a hospital institutionalizes the control of a disease like cancer. *If only our organization could get some of that cancer money,* she thought.

Her mind drifted back to that bed, and the smell, the warmth of the man she had left behind so she could go to work. She sighed and read through the reports on the screen and waited for her break.

People shuffled in and out of that room from all walks of life. Every once in a while, she would see a suit brush by her or see a student from her school, and she would hide the shock. She really didn't understand this world she lived in at all. Feeling small in light of it all didn't embarrass her like she thought it would; she felt enlightened by it. For so long, she had been taught to know all the right answers. She had forgotten how precious it is to wonder and to not have all the answers. To learn for its own sake. Earlier today, she had been afraid to come to work. Now she was grateful that she had. She had been given a new vision to see with – one she never could have gotten anywhere else.

28

AFTER THAT NIGHT ON DUNDAS CHARLES' LIFE WENT BACK TO NORMAL for him. He stopped watching the news and reading the papers waiting to be caught. He wasn't going to be caught. He was just going to go back to school every day and help with the funerals like before. He would play Xbox at night with Jonathon online, but it wasn't the same. He fell into a groove that all young people fall into with school. It was feast or famine. He would study relentlessly and get the best grades he could while not having much money or time for extracurricular activities besides Xbox. Then when classes were done, he would work like crazy and earn as much money as he could, while spending it all at the same time.

The funerals became second nature to him. He even began cremating and embalming with Robert in the basement. The Pinketts were getting old, and they both were starting to show it. Charles was having to do more night pick-ups and extra things that the Pinkett's used to do with ease. They leaned on him more and more for help. Jonathon came home to help sometimes in the summers, but he had recently started his internship, so he would be staying in Boston and couldn't come home. Charles was only twenty-one years old, but he knew the business like the back of his hand now. He had been certified in 2018, and now he took care of most of the heavy lifting for the Pinkett's.

The funerals Charles prepared were mostly for older people who had died. They were the business' bread and butter. His first cremation was an older woman, and his first embalmment was an older gentleman. He was always respectful of the deceased like he was dealing with his own parents. He thought of them a lot while he was at work. He liked the job because he was able to meet his clients at a level that he mostly operated on anyway. When his parents died, he never came all the way back from that. The veil had been lifted, and he saw the world for what it truly was: heartbreakingly beautiful. He adored the flowers that were always fresh and respected the dearly departed that were waiting downstairs. The only funerals that didn't sit well for him was when a young person passed. There was no "they lived a good life"; it was mostly shrieking silence and confusion.

The overdose funerals were his least favorite. Nobody is prepared for an overdose funeral and half the crowd that comes to view the body is stoned themselves. The bathroom was always occupied during the overdose services, and the crowd was hostile. He felt for the families. They never seemed to deserve their fate, but the bodies downstairs were bleached white with dark black lips and were grotesque to him. The track marks and the scars were everywhere. Teenagers and young adults weren't so bad. They always drew a huge crowd with a mostly respectful audience, but the older crowd saw empty rooms that seemed to fill with ghosts.

Charles was afraid of these people. Some would leave their carts outside or a sleeping bag near the door. Some refused to leave after the service, and they would have to call the police. Charles sat through those funerals feeling edgy. On one night in particular, there was a viewing for a man whose family spent a fortune making him look presentable. The house was full of ghosts and the family. Charles wore his somber but helpful persona and stood by the door.

He was approached out of the crowd by a man who looked disheveled and lost. "Hey, is there anywhere I can get some water?" he asked.

"Yeah, of course," Charles replied and led the man into a mostly empty room where they were serving refreshments.

"Some spread," the man said to Charles, grabbing a water and a plate of food.

Charles kept his distance from the man who seemed to have changed his demeanor since leaving the other room. "Yeah, they wanted everyone to be comfortable, considering," Charles replied like he had said it a hundred times.

"Hey, I remember you now. You're that cop's kid. Yeah, I remember. You were here for that funeral too. You work here now?" the man said curiously.

"Yeah, I stayed on after. The Pinketts have been good to me," Charles replied, looking away from the man.

"I'm Casper," he said putting out his hand. When Charles shook the man's hand, he was pulled close. "I know what you did," he hissed and Charles pulled back in a fright.

"What is that supposed to mean?" Charles retorted angrily, dusting his suit off and looking around.

"It wasn't professional, and you could tell it was amateur night, but it was well executed all the same," the man said looking around the room.

"What?" Charles said confused.

"Some time ago, down the way you left that junkie Singy lying in a pool of his own blood. I commend you. There were a lot of pissed off people after that. Lots of people wanted a piece of that rat."

Charles felt extremely uncomfortable and scared. He started looking at the exits so he could run when the man put his hand on Charles' shoulder and said, "Hey, I'm not trying to lecture you. I admire the work. I felt bad when your father went down. I wish I could have gutted that junkie myself. We got him though. And now you are helping us without even knowing it." The man patted Charles again and took a sip of water.

Charles was silent and terrified by the mention of the incident, and he wanted to leave.

"Hey, if you ever want to do that again, we got lots of room for a man like you," said the man as he handed Charles a card with a number on it. As he made for the door, Charles was left standing there as if he had seen a ghost.

Charles felt as though his whole world had been flipped upside-down that night. He thought nobody was going to find out. He was scared and intrigued by the offer. He couldn't stop thinking about it.

He called the number two weeks later and left a message. Nobody phoned him back. He had almost forgotten about the ordeal when he was walking home one night and heard a voice behind him.

"Hello, Charles. How's life been treating you?" was all he heard.

When he turned around, he saw Casper leaning up against an alleyway entrance. Charles hadn't noticed him as he walked by.

"Hey," Charles said looking around.

"Let's take a walk," Casper said motioning Charles into the alley. He must have followed Casper for ten minutes through different alleyways he had never seen and across streets he didn't recognize before they finally stopped. Casper looked around an abandoned parking lot overlooking a park and said, "I came to you because I see a great destiny before you, Charles. I see all that you could be, and I'm excited for you."

Charles looked around cautiously and then looked back at Casper. "I don't understand," Charles said.

"Do you believe that everything that happened to you has happened by chance, or do you feel that it was deliberate?" Casper asked.

"I don't know. I'm not religious, if that's what you're asking," Charles said back.

"How could you be?" Casper said with a scoff. "I love this city, Charles, but it is going to hell fast, and not in a religious sense."

Charles observed a silence between them and waited.

"I'm going to tell you who we are and then you can either come with us or go your own way, but let me be clear: Once I've told you, I cannot un-tell you, understand?" Casper said forcefully.

"Okay," Charles answered.

Casper took a deep breath and started in on it. "Historically, societies have been built on checks and balances. We restore that balance. You could say we do the jobs that the politicians and constituents don't know how to do ask for but need just as much as water and clean air. We provide justice. If you are given this life and all it has to offer, with all its beauty and tragedy, If you are endowed with that life and you decide to squander it, and you sell your soul to the pipe and the rig and trapse around this city begging, stealing, and robbing, you are going to be taken. Maybe not today and maybe not tomorrow, but eventually we will find you. That is what I'm offering you. To be your father's son and rid this city of the very people who destroyed your family."

As Casper said this, the whole crown chakra around the halo of Charles' head electrified. It was like a door had opened. The world had seemed so frivolous and uncaring, so bland and tasteless before he heard those words. Charles took a deep breath and looked up at a cloudy sky and spotted one star peering out from behind the veil of clouds.

"Okay, I'm in," Charles answered. It was the first time in a long time that he felt he was taking control of his life. He had existed so passively that he hadn't even known he was alive until he killed that junkie in the street. After that, he felt alive, like his life mattered and theirs didn't. No more homeless paradise. No more junkie utopia.

29

AMY WOKE IN THE MIDDLE OF THE NIGHT SWEATING. SHE COULDN'T shake the news of the coming epidemic. This dope was going to send the city into a tailspin. She drank a coffee at two in the morning and searched the web for veterinarians she could talk to. She read and read about xylazine, benzo, and fentanyl until her eyes felt like they were bleeding. She fell back asleep at 6:30 a.m., only to wake at 8:00 a.m. She took a shower and made herself a breakfast shake and a coffee before she got on the phone.

She looked out at a motionless world since the lockdown began. She felt like a house cat. She dialed the number and waited for a response.

"Hello," a deep voice answered.

"Hello, Doctor Reeves. This is Amy Winter with the Coroner's office. I wondered if I could have a word with you this morning."

"Okay," he said wearily.

"I wanted to know what you know about xylazine," Amy asked quickly.

"Well, it's a tranquilizer for horses mostly; we use it on them when they need dental work and other surgical procedures," Reeves answered reflexively.

"Are you aware that humans mix it into drugs?" Amy asked.

"Well, yes, I have heard that," he said with a sigh.

"I was wondering if you knew of anything we could use to reverse the effects of it in humans?" Amy asked.

"Well, the two largest adrenergic agonist reversers are tolazoline and yohimbine," he answered.

"Can we use them on humans, though?" Amy asked again.

"Yes, we do use it on humans in small amounts, but you might need more than a small amount," Reeves answered.

"Let me put it this way. Say people are using it in heroin and the Narcan isn't reversing the effects of the xylazine, and people were dying. Could we use it to reverse the effects of the xylazine?" Amy asked.

"Well, as you know, I'm not a human doctor, but given the circumstances, I would say that using tolazoline in small doses – like 0.4 mgs at a time up to the amount of 2.0 mgs – would possibly reverse the effects. Yohimbine is much more potent in small doses. It has been linked to the majority of horse deaths in rare cases where horses die after being given it when there were complications with xylazine. I will mention that tolazoline also has been involved in the deaths of horses during complications with the use of xylazine but only half as often. It's a gamble," Reeves said taking a deep breath.

"One last question, doctor?" Amy asked.

"Yes?" Reeves replied.

"What was the dose you gave the horses," Amy asked.

"Four milligrams to reverse the effects," Reeves answered.

"Thank you for your time," Amy finished with as she hung up the phone. She sent an email stating her intentions to Ahmed down at the lab and waited for his response. In the meantime, she typed up a proposal to the health authority and the mayor's office. Just then Ahmed gave her the green light and she pressed send on the proposals to both offices simultaneously. She leaned back and waited for a shit storm of controversy and red tape, but she knew she had found a Hail Mary in the last moments of the game.

30

Mikah came into work that morning in a daze. She had been working twelve hour shifts for a couple months, and instead of getting used to them, she was being worn down by them. She saw dead people and imagined seeing people overdosing everywhere she went. When she sat at the computer that morning, Perry gave her a sideways look. "What?" Mikah said taking a sip of her coffee.

Perry shook his head and said, "Good morning, how are you feeling?"

"I'm alright," she answered passively. She scrolled through the reports looking for anything to distract her from his gaze. She felt like he was staring right through her.

"Are you starting to see our clients everywhere yet?" Perry asked.

"What?" Mikah asked.

"The participants and the deceased – are you starting to see them everywhere yet?" Perry pressed.

"A little, yeah. How did you know?" Mikah said with relief and fright mixed together, elevating her awareness of her surroundings suddenly. The room seemed to get brighter, and she began to feel lighter.

"Well, we all see it. It's just we all don't last," Perry said looking down the line of booths. "This job is a killer," he said with a sigh.

"I see those people from the other day every time I walk in a door. I picture them on the ground, and I have to start loading shots, but they die anyway," she said.

"Yeah, I've seen a lot of that," Perry said.

Mikah exhaled a breath she didn't know she was holding in. The next few minutes would change the way she viewed her job forever.

Perry looked off into the distance and said, "It reminds me of the talks I used to have with Vietnam Veterans. You see in Vietnam, they were waging what could only be described as a mechanical war. They had the draft in the US, which meant that they had an unlimited supply of material to throw at the enemy. There was the navy, army, and air force all competing to meet quotas that were put out by the pentagon. The objective was to produce kills from each arm of the forces. You actually had men walking around a battlefield after a fight, counting body parts on a clip board.

"The kills were allocated to different departments for their quotas. If you were on the ground, and you didn't meet your quota of kills, you would be shipped more supplies and water, but you weren't allowed to return to base. The infantry would kill anything that moved to come back to base. To make matters worse, you had to share the kills with anyone who helped you. If you didn't give proper stats to the air force or navy, you might not get air cover next time. The war was being run like an assembly line at a car plant, with a never-ending supply of cheap steel in the form of the draft.

"Now why I say this is that I see all you students come out of school with your caring degrees, and I can't tell the difference between your graduation and the draft. There are no jobs in your fields because those jobs really don't exist for you – just like being a hero didn't exist in Vietnam in the way it did in WWII. Soldiers were sold the idea of heroism being like killing Nazis, but when they got to Vietnam and were killing children and farmers in the jungle, they were disillusioned. The same way you guys are taught that the world shouldn't be a certain way, and then you come out here expecting to make a difference, but you realize that this is a culture too, just like yours, and it got this way the same way yours did.

"This is a school too, if you haven't noticed, but it's life and death here. The stakes are higher, and nobody gets the summer off. The point of this operation we are in is to get overdoses, in the same way the US army collected 'kills'. If we produce more overdoses, we get more funding – just like how the shelter gets more funding if it has a higher volume of clients. This is the war on drugs and homelessness. It's called outreach, but it's the exact opposite because we can throw away the newly graduated in the same way they could throw away soldiers in Vietnam because of the draft. This job is the new canon, and the recently graduated student are the ammo.

"The most obvious thing about it is that none of these agencies talk to each other. In a war, you need good communication lines, or you will lose. Nobody talks to each other across agencies. How can you win a war without open communication and cooperation? You can't. So, what I see is that this situation isn't built to succeed, it's built to fail. What we are doing down here is poverty perpetuation and management. This is the opposite of harm reduction; it's harm perpetuation and management.

"We are not losing the war; we lost it a long time ago. It's a business based on funding and funding comes from volume. Volume comes from losing. Volume comes from looking the other way from the top down, and anytime it looks like our efforts are working, you cut the funding and it all goes back to zero. Every place in the country had their numbers skyrocket last year, and I'll bet every one of them was making headway in their districts the year before.

"This is inverted war. Instead of recovering and stabilizing being the main goal, it is destabilization and overdosing that is the desired effect. The system is rigged to destroy the newcomer through disillusionment, overwork and no benefits or sick days for when you get burned out. Portugal has decriminalized and medicalized its approach to drug addiction. They had three overdose deaths per million last year. In 2020, everyone's numbers doubled! Portugal had thirty overdose deaths out of ten million people. We had thirty six deaths in our city alone in January, and we have a population of five million. This is by design." Perry looked down at his feet and couldn't look Mikah in the eyes.

She stared back at him in wonder and no longer felt ashamed for the way she felt. She felt enlightened. She felt a sense of self-protection coming back to her. She no longer felt open. She felt guarded, as if instantly, she mattered too, just like the people she was helping, but more. The codependency bled away from her vision, and she took a deep breath. "Thank you," was all she could say.

Perry patted her on the back and said, "Don't mention it…no, seriously." He motioned to Susan's office, and they both laughed. Mikah felt more like herself for the first time in about a month. She sat back and absorbed the stories but didn't go down with them. She observed but didn't participate. She felt self-actualization take the place of depression, and she found that they were the same thing. The morning flew by after that, and she didn't look back.

31

THE FIRST TIME THAT CHARLES MET UP WITH CASPER AFTER THEIR FIRST meeting was late at night on East Dundas Street, just past the funeral home. They just walked around back alleys and side streets. Casper studied the homeless sleeping bundled up tight to keep out the cold. He handed out cigarettes to some and money to others, but every once and a while, he handed someone a pipe and a small bag with a tinged yellow rock in it and say, "For your pain." Then the two would walk around for another hour and double back to the person, and Casper would collect his pipe and walk away. There wasn't any violence to it. No malice or rage. It looked like mercy to Charles.

He followed Casper on those cold nights and watched how Casper operated. He could have been a preacher in another life. He was kind and thoughtful; he remembered people's names and faces. He played both sides of the fence. Sometimes when they gave out a package, they wouldn't double back. Charles would ask why, and Casper would say, "Stagger your collection. Always do five times more for people than the collection is worth. If you're going to take one, you gotta raise a few up. Plant five times as many seeds as the soul you pick," Casper would say.

Charles came to understand that the city streets are like a jungle with a natural habitat. If you take from it without disturbing the balance of things, you can always take more, but if you took too rapidly without foresight, you would meet with resistance and sideways looks. People would remember you, and they would talk. You had to be visible but invisible to memory. "The boat ride isn't far for the ones we take.

Everything on this plain has already forgotten them when we come for them," Casper would say.

It took about a month before Charles handed out his first pipe and package. His hands shook, but he kept his composure. His heart pounded the whole hour they walked around and doubled back. When they came back to that man tucked in his sleeping bag, he had passed, pipe clutched in his hand. Charles slid the pipe from his hand and walked off into the night. He felt a wave of exhilaration replace his fear. He searched Casper's face for some kind of recognition, and he saw it shining back at him. He wanted to hold that moment close forever. He thought about his parents and just let it all go. For those moments, late at night out in the pitch black, they were the lions of the Toronto plains.

32

AMY READ THROUGH THE RESPONSES TO HER PLAN AND NODDED HER head in agreement. She was waiting for a big fight, but once she explained that they could have up to ten overdose deaths a day from this dope, they all fell in line. She had already ordered fifteen thousand 0.4 shots of tolazoline. The protocol was in place. Once a person was unresponsive to three shots of 0.4 mgs of Narcan and a nasal, which was equivalent to ten shots, they would be given the Hail Mary shot of up to 5 units of 0.4 tolazoline. She sent the order to the health authority and awaited the arrival of the shipment. She only hoped that they got them in time.

33

THE DAY BEFORE THE HAIL MARY SHOTS ARRIVED, THEY HAD THEIR FIRST taste of what was to come. In one day, in the suburbs, they had ten overdose deaths of people who were all administered Narcan but died anyway. There were five deaths downtown. Fear swept the city. As if the streets weren't empty enough during the lockdown, they dried up fast after that.

Amy was just sending the Hail Mary packages out to injection sites, camps, and community centers when the next wave began. They had five more overdose deaths in a matter of hours. It was pandemonium. The ambulances and fire trucks started running twenty-four hours a day. The numbers they were looking to slow in COVID deaths were replaced in overdose deaths. The safe supply initiative was drained in days. The news shifted from the COVID case count to stories about dead people lying in the streets and in the camps. It was biblical.

Amy was in touch with all the places where she had sent the doses and waited for the updates to come back with her jaw clenched and her eyes watering. She got her first call sometime around 6:00 p.m., after a litany of tragic calls from all over the city. The Hail Mary had worked in three different cases in the North End. She clapped her hands loudly and then cried into them. *This might work,* she thought as she looked at the pictures of her daughters on her desk.

34

WHEN MIKAH CAME INTO WORK THAT MORNING, THEY HAD A STAFF meeting. "Okay, listen up," Susan said, putting her weight on her back leg and her hands together softly in front of her. "I know stakes are high after the day we had yesterday. Luckily, we have not had any of the bad dope here yet. Today, we have a package from the Health Authority that might just save the day. These shots in the light blue bottles are 0.4 shots of what they are calling the 'Hail Mary shot'. It's called tolazoline and it reverses the xylazine in the fentanyl.

"As a last resort, after you have administered three shots of Narcan and up to the equivalent of a nasal, she looked directly at Mikah when she said it "you then administer to the nonresponsive person up to five shots of the Hail Mary. You will only have five in your kit, so you won't get confused. Work together and save some lives today," she said in a resounding voice towards the end.

Perry looked over across the room and said, "Let's open up."

Tdot was the first through the door, and K-ultra followed behind him. The two seperated into their respective booths far away from each other.

Everyone else who came in wanted their dope checked. "You guys get your dope checked?" Perry asked K-ultra, and he nodded. "I don't buy from those creepy fucks" he said as he lit the bottom of his cooker and stared through the flame at his reflection in the mirror and stuck his tongue out. He was sweating profusely.

Tdot set up his shot and smashed quick. He turned around rubbing his arm and said, "They did this on purpose."

"Who did?" Mikah asked.

"The ghosts," he whispered.

"Shut up, cunt," K-ultra yelled from the other end of the room.

"Why would anybody do this on purpose?" Mikah asked.

"To finish their plan of wiping us all out. They are trying to end homelessness," Tdot said, rolling his eyes.

"Good luck with that shit; not with these housing prices, I'm going to be homeless soon," Perry interjected.

"Who are these ghosts?" Mikah asked looking at Perry.

Perry looked down the booths. "They think they control the balance. They kill anyone weak or new," he said crossing his arms.

"Why doesn't anybody do anything about it?" Mikah asked.

"Because it's always been that way," K-ultra said throwing the rig out in front of him with two fingers. "This isn't *Alice in Wonderland*. In our world, the Red Queen always wins, and she is always taking heads – just like these ghosts or the bikers or the Chinese or the Jamaicans, and on and on ad infinitum," he said rubbing his arm and staring at the ceiling.

Mikah felt scared for everyone she saw. *How could they survive?* she thought.

After a few moments of leaning against his booth, Tdot finally said, "Could you play 'Ride the Lightning' by Metallica?" Mikah nodded.

"This fucking guy," K-ultra said with a laugh.

"Shut up, goof, or maybe I won't save your life tonight," Tdot said winking at Mikah.

"Who, you calling a goof? Cunt!" K-ultra yelled.

"Who you calling a cunt? Bird!" Tdot returned.

Just then, Mikah turned up the volume, and they both went back to their high. She listened to the heavy guitar and looked at her own reflection in the mirror. The day had begun.

"Here guys, take these Hail Mary kits with you," Perry said, putting them in the booths.

"Yeah, Yeah," K-ultra returned.

35

IT WAS ALMOST A YEAR INTO CHARLES' APPRENTICESHIP BEFORE HE WAS invited to come to a gathering. "There is a warehouse. It isn't close to the city, nor is it far. It resides over the highway, off of the road known as Don Way in the industrial park, where the smell of iron and freight fill the air." Charles came alone. When he walked in, he could see an altar and long line of people. He stood in line and waited his turn. When he got to the front, he put his glass pipes in the chalice that was lined with thin wire and ash. He then followed the person in front of him, and they stood side by side, facing the altar. He didn't look left or right, he just waited.

After the last clink of glass came from the bottom of the cage, and the last shadow moved into the line, the chalice was placed on the altar. A large propane tank was sparked, producing an incandescent light that raged beneath. The figure at the altar grabbed a steel pipe and broke the glass by dropping the heavy end into the basket repeatedly. A funnel of smoke traveled upwards, making a tunnel of light and smoke as it made its way to the heavens. The man removed his hands from his pockets and dropped handfuls of coins into the amber flames beneath him. The room erupted in cheers.

The man pulled back his cloak, and there before them stood Casper. "Good evening, brothers. I see you have all been busy," and they all laughed. "I welcome you all here this evening. Tonight, we welcome a young man to our brotherhood who needs no introduction. You should have felt his presence long ago. You know of him, and tonight we make him one of our own. Come forth son and receive thy prize," Casper said motioning him forward.

When Charles was standing in front of the altar, Casper put his hands forward and said a prayer that Charles had never heard before. "Though we walk the earth among you, we are not one of you; though we walk the earth, we are not of the earth. You cannot see our wings. You cannot see what the night brings. The night is ours and ours alone. We keep it safe until the saviour comes home."

Charles felt electrified by the words, and a tear rolled down his cheek.

"You are home," Casper said, and the whole room started to clap a thunderous melody by clapping and stomping feet simultaneously. The very ground shook. Charles was surrounded by the thunder, and then he felt the pats on his back come from all his brothers. He was enveloped in a cloak of safety and purpose. He would never look back or away again. He would take the brotherhood to new levels given his natural talents.

The years passed by like that. Charon became the legend bestowed upon him. He made people disappear across the River Styx and into the land of the dead. There were whispers that he turned them to ash and spread them in the river. Some said he took the bodies to the beaver lakes up north, where not even a bone was left behind. The legend built up around him like nobody before, and once he was old enough, he was chosen to lead the chapter into the age of pandemic. They used the cities' fear against them and wreaked a havoc like none seen before. 2020 was their year. Nobody could deny it, if they knew about it – but the greatest trick the devil ever pulled was convincing the world he didn't exist.

36

MIKAH WAS ACCUSTOMED TO COMING OVER ON THE WEEKENDS BECAUSE Charles was working nights all week. She got used to the smell of formaldehyde and sulphur that blanketed the lower rooms. When she got upstairs, all she could smell was freshly baked bread and the Pinketts' wonderful coffee. She felt the love that exuded from every door upstairs in that house. She often sat in the living room and studied all the books up there: Mythology, history, poetry, and loads of magazines from a different time it seemed. She would flip through old catalogues and gasp at the price differences. "An oven was thirty dollars," she would say to herself.

It wasn't long before she would hear a large figure coming up the stairs. She could feel his arms around her before they even embraced. That month had been hard for her. She didn't know what she would have done if she didn't have him by her side. He would come and sit beside her on the couch and kiss her face and then carry her "up in the air" in his arms into his bedroom when nobody was around. He laid her on the bed so gently that she felt she was lying on a cloud. He kissed her more times than she could count, and she trembled in his presence. She hadn't told anyone about him. He was still her secret.

She looked into his eyes in the afterglow and dreamed of all the places she wanted to go with him. His eyes wandered though. He was captivated by something in the distance, but she couldn't tell what. She was turned on by his sometimes mysterious nature. How could he be so strong given all that he had been through? How could he be so gentle? She felt it sometimes in the throes of passion. She could feel a large force being dispelled. She loved absorbing his energy; God knows, he absorbed hers.

She left unsaid all her wonders about him and just enjoyed what they had. She thought often of their first date at the Whitney block and how she would like to go there again. She had so many new curiosities about it. She would ask questions, and Charles would give her long speeches about the tower and the city then. He wanted them to fix the tower and use it again, but at the same time, he loved the ghostly symbol it had become.

They fell asleep in each other's arms and drifted away, beyond time and space, beyond the city and all its pain. They drifted off into that day when all the cherry blossoms were budding, and all the possibilities of the world lay before them. The weekend always slipped away so fast – faster than she could chase it. She always wanted one more night with him before they had to return to their lives. She was full of want when he was around, no matter how much she got. He was an addicting force in her life. She loved her hunger for him. She hoped it would never pass.

37

AMY READ THROUGH VARIOUS REPORTS FROM DIFFERENT SERVICE PROviders; the Hail Mary dose was making serious headway in the suburbs. It was even working downtown. The overdose rate had spiked at first, but then with the use of the new safe supply measures and the Hail Mary shot, it had mostly leveled off. She felt elated, and she was being congratulated every time she picked up the phone. She had even been asked to talk directly with the premier, been interviewed for TV news and the newspapers.

The city was now embracing both around-the-clock COVID vaccinations and the Hail Mary protocol, as it had been dubbed in the news. The threat had not completely gone away, and the dope was still testing heavy with xylazine, but she felt she had more control over what was happening than just catching the tail end of a tornado. She felt as though she was in the eye of the storm, which gave her some foresight on where to go next.

As she was sipping on her coffee, waiting for her daughters to get up, she started reading through a letter that was found on the body of a suspected suicide at Trinity Bellwood Park. The young woman had written the following:

> All my friends have been stolen from me. I woke and they were gone.
>
> What COVID and Down left behind was stolen from me in the night. Nobody believes me. Nobody Cares. I saw the man with blue eyes.
>
> I saw him and No One Cares.

Amy felt chills run up her spine. As the Coroner, one of Amy's jobs was to record the last day of someone's life. She usually compiled the playlist the person was listening to; the searches they made on their phone; posts they made; people they talked to. With this girl, she didn't have much. She decided to go to Trinity Bellwood Park herself and look at the tent the young woman had died in.

Trinity Bellwood Park was the largest camp out of the 120 camps in the city since the pandemic began. It has been described as a "nice neighborhood" because of the people that lived near the camp. Campers felt safe there. When Amy arrived, it looked abandoned. There was all sorts of debris on the ground: dolls, mattresses, and all sorts of children's jewelry. Garbage was everywhere. Amy walked over to the tent with yellow caution tape around it and looked inside. You could see an old blanket and food wrappers inside. The floor was wet, and it smelled musty. She leaned down in front and sifted through the belongings there. It was the same as the photo she had in the file, but the smell and the actual sight of the surroundings made her heart sink.

This girl was 22. The water lining the edges of the tent glimmered at her, and she zipped the tent back up. She couldn't take it. She stood up and began walking towards the car, when she saw a man knelt down in front of his tent, configuring a bike crank. He looked at her as she walked by. Amy stopped in her tracks and asked, "Did you know anything about the girl who passed recently?"

"Sadie was a nice girl," he said staring through the crank in his hands as if he were the only one there.

"Did she have any friends I could talk to?" Amy asked.

"She was all alone in this world," he said spinning the crank.

"What do you mean?" Amy asked.

He put the crank down and said, "Her world was taken from her, one night at a time, just like the rest of them." He rummaged underneath himself for something he had lost but couldn't find.

"What?" Amy asked again.

"Sometimes they go home, sometimes they go west, and sometimes they go away like the rest," he said looking to the sky.

"What rest?" Amy asked.

The man looked back at the ground and drew a blank look. He searched his mind for an answer and finally, he took a deep breath and said, "No one cares. They are here one day and gone the next. No one cares," he repeated.

"Where have they gone?" Amy asked.

"Across the river and no one cares," he repeated.

Amy walked away and started driving back to her house. *Across the river?* she thought. *They are here one day and gone the next?* Ahmed said he thought the bodies in the river were put there by some ferryman. There were reports of missing people, more and more every day, but most people had left the city, searching for answers somewhere else. She racked her brain as she drove through the streets and past the camps, the vaccine sites, and empty streets since the shutdown had begun.

If you were going to take people, now would be the best time. distractions, restrictions, and scared people. What river is there to take people over in Toronto? Is it just a saying or is there a place? A place where nobody goes? Where nobody can see? She started to take deep breaths. She could feel it in her gut, but she had to be sure. She went home and pulled out a map of the city...

38

IN THE DARK OF NIGHT, SITTING ON A BENCH IN A DIMLY LIT PARK, SAT Dax. At his feet lay the body of a young man no older than 20 years old. His face was white, and his lips were blue. Dax was holding three pre-ready shots in one hand and a nasal in the other. He scanned the park for movement and then looked back down at the body coldly.

What a waste, he thought. Just then, the boy gave out a deep gargling gasp. It filled the air with his breath. Dax leaned forward and gave him a nasal in each nostril and waited. Once it was apparent that the nasal didn't work, Dax gave him three shots of the Hail Mary, alternating between legs, and waited. He scanned the park again this time with more intensity. He watched as the color came back in the young man's eyes, and he began to take panicked breaths. Within moments, his eyes were darting left to right.

Dax lit a smoke and stepped over the body. "You're lucky," he said over his shoulder as he caned his way to the entrance of the park. *It does work*, he thought to himself as he felt his purpose receding like the night into morning. He felt small and ineffectual again. All that planning, testing, and waiting had all gone up in smoke. Dax thought back to all the people he had tested his serum on over the years and how this was the culmination of many near attempts. He for once had a batch that was reliable, Narcan-proof, ambulance-proof, and even hospital-proof. He shook his head as he stumbled and caught his breath up against a wall on Dundas Street.

"Am I losing my touch? Is it over?" he asked himself. He didn't quite know yet, but he would lay low and wait for a plan to formalize.

39

MIKAH WAS ON EDGE ALL WEEK AT WORK. THE STORIES SHE HEARD ABOUT deaths everywhere was enough to have her feeding off of her own body chemistry. She was bleeding her adrenalin dry in four-hour intervals. She drank a lot of coffee to offset the low feeling. Yet they never had one overdose in the unit when she was there; they never used one Hail Mary shot. It was confusing. She just chalked it up to drug testing and shaky participants. She surfed the internet and listened to the participants as she actively played requests for music. The music ranged from Tool to Metallica, then Drake to Tupac, and then every once in a while, Madonna. They all got along pretty well in the shadow of the storm.

Perry even seemed relieved. By the time her week was done, she couldn't wait to climb the stairs at Charles' house and wrap herself in him and sleep until she couldn't sleep any longer. These twelve-hour shifts were killing her. She would work three in a row, but they were always short-staffed, so she worked four sometimes. The energy she made seeped out of her as fast as her body made it. Being on that plane was like being inside a vacuum. Nothing survived, everything was drained.

She dreamt of sleep and Charles' constantly. She rushed to him and caught him waking up. "Hello, darling," he would say as he lay back down and put out his arms to her. She would slide into them and let go, all the way down she would go. She hoped those moments with him would never end. Love in such a chaotic time made no sense to her, but she was grateful for it. He smelled so good. She was in a trance when she was enveloped in him. She would do anything he said.

The two of them drifted off to sleep after only leaving the room for bare necessities. Charles told her of his nights moving COVID bodies from the morgue to mass graves outside the city. Mikah thought her job was hard. She listened to him and studied his face. He wore no trauma, no regret. He looked fulfilled despite the grainy nature of his existence. He was an undertaker essentially. He dealt mostly with dead people, but it didn't seem to wear on him. She envied that. She told him of the dramas of her work and her building trauma. He was sympathetic. He listened and added comments. He cared deeply for her. She could feel it, but she couldn't feel any of his trauma. He seemed superhuman to her.

"Maybe I could come with you some night?" Mikah asked him. She was hoping he would rub off on her somehow. Seeing a man at work was one of her greatest turn-ons. She didn't mention that.

"Well, you're not really authorized, but I think we might be able to make an exception," Charles said kissing her on the forehead.

40

AMY SEARCHED MAP AFTER MAP FOR RIVERS THAT COULD BE USED BY THE killers. She started with the Don River, given that both bodies were dumped in different parts of it. *But they weren't carried across it,* she thought as she searched the river. *To cross the Don River from the homeless camps, you would have to be heading east. If these bodies were being taken from the city over a river to the east, we would have to start looking in places like Scarborough, which made sense given its strategic drug trade connection with downtown, but Scarborough doesn't have anywhere to bury people.*

She looked at the Green River, but it didn't ring true. *If they wanted to get rid of large amounts of bodies, they must be mortuary savvy,* she thought. *I mean how do you make people disappear without a trace without knowing where bodies are buried? Without anyone seeing you? You would have to be hiding in plain sight. Where were poor people buried in the past? Wellington County or Norfolk County.*

What if the person is in the business? Why else would they place the coins for the ferryman if they weren't in the business somehow. This is highly orchestrated, and I can't see this being some amateur. These people love history and mythology. What river runs between here and Wellington County? Norfolk is too far, she thought.

There is the Credit River that starts in Mississauga. The Humber River that starts downtown. She looked at the Wellington burial plots and saw that they were using a facility and plot there to bury unclaimed bodies infected with COVID. Her whole body started to shake. She looked at the river closest to the old Wellington County burial grounds called the "poor house" and she knew. *The Grand River, the largest river in southern*

Ontario. It all fell in place for her then. *These people work for some kind of burial service downtown or know somebody who does. They could have been contracted out by the city morgue to transfer our bodies there. They could be carrying bodies of their own and mixing them in with ours.*

It was perfect. Nobody would disturb them or ask questions about the bodies. Paperwork could always be forged or digitally notarized. Those facilities dealt with very few people inside a very tight knit industry. The people bringing bodies there were heroes; they would never be questioned. She sat back and took it all in. What if the overdoses were just a distraction? Who would believe her?

She called Ahmed down at the morgue. "Hello," he answered. You could hear the sound of the saw in the background. She could hear him stepping away.

"Hey, who do we have transporting COVID bodies that have been interred?" she asked.

"Well, only one right now. Young guy named Charles. He is part of the Pinketts on East Dundas, why?" Ahmed asked.

"How often?" she asked with adrenalin pumping through her veins.

"Well, you know we can't store the bodies here for the unidentified because of the protocols. Let me see, twice a week, but he has to do multiple runs when we have waves of deliveries. Things are backed up. He is running every night, five days a week, all night. The guy's a machine," Ahmed said.

Amy almost dropped the phone. Her mouth opened wide, and she took a deep breath. She put her hand over her mouth to stop herself from reacting.

"What's the problem?" Ahmed asked after the silence.

"That is lots. No, just wondering. I saw some of these expense reports, and I was just following up. Thank you. I'll let you get back to work," she said as professionally as she could.

"Okay, talk soon," and he hung up.

Amy's heart was pumping as she scrolled through her contacts. She couldn't contact Detective Mason because she didn't trust him. How could he not know about the xylazine connection if it had been going on for a year, if they weren't in on it somehow? It wasn't above these city cops to be confiscating the dope and selling it themselves. She couldn't risk a tip off before she knew for sure.

She did know a surveillance unit captain, named John Sullivan, that she dated years ago after her husband had died, but he was married, and she never felt good about it, so she ended it. He would be able to tell her what to do. She texted him and said, "This is business," and waited for a reply. This was the thinnest evidence she had ever seen, but it was coming together.

If she could follow that kid for a couple weeks with a GPS tracker, that would be all the evidence she needed for real resources to be thrown that way. She waited for the text, biting her fingernails to the quick. All those old feelings started to come back as she waited for the text. She thought about how fast they had hooked up and how serious it felt, then it was over. Waiting for the text made her feel like no time had passed. It was hard. She went to bed that night with no reply from him.

41

WHEN MIKAH GOT TO WORK ON MONDAY, SHE SETTLED IN AND CHECKED the shift reports from the weekend. It was the strangest thing: They had six overdose events and used the Hail Mary every time. She felt jealous somehow. She never got to use it, and there were no overdoses during her shifts. She was grateful, but she still lacked purpose when there wasn't. It was a strange dichotomy to be party to. She was here to reduce overdoses but needed them to feel useful. It was like a paramedic waiting for a call. When you don't get a lot of calls, you don't make the kind of money you would like, and you are devoid of purpose.

Every once in a while, a slow part of the river is appreciated, but not days and days of it. The action part of the job was starting to run in her veins. The tragedy and the ecstasy of being on the edge of life and death was intoxicating. She craved it and was terrified of it all at once. She wondered where the longing had come from. She was always such a planner before this. Now she was actively awaiting the complete spontaneity of overdose drama. Just then, she was interrupted by K-ultra and T dot coming through the waiting room.

"Just smash and let's go you, fuckin idiot," Tdot said as K-ultra went to the farthest booth he could find.

"We might get a car today," Tdot said with a gleam in his eye.

"Are you going to sell it?" Mikah asked.

"Fuck no, we are going to live in it," he said proudly. "No more, moldy tent action. Nobody is taking us in our sleep," T dot finished.

"Who takes people in their sleep?" Mikah asked with surprise.

"Shut up you, fuckin' rat goof!" K-ultra yelled from his booth.

"Shut up and hurry up. I'm having a conversation with my friend," T dot said turning to Mikah. "I don't know really, but lots of empty tents are out there with people's stuff still in them. Vanished like ghosts," Tdot said with fear in his voice.

"I'm done," K-ultra said as he put the rig in the container hanging off the wall in his booth.

"Let's go then, fuck nuts," Tdot yelled. He had disturbed a couple of other booths that were all yelling at them to get out. They left as swiftly as they came in, and the room fell back into the groove.

Mikah looked over at Perry and asked, "Do you believe that?" she asked.

"I believe that there is a lot going on right now that I can't explain, and like I said before, since last year, I know dozens of people missing. No word, no goodbye, and their stuff still being kept by people," Perry said with a sigh. "As long as these restrictions stay tight, our population down here will get the worst of it. These restrictions don't take these people into account at all. It's a 'save yourself' mentality." Perry stepped out for a smoke after that. Mikah scrolled down the computer screen looking at the faces of all the missing person posters. Then she stood up and stretched her legs after that and walked around.

42

WHEN AMY WOKE UP, SHE STILL DIDN'T HAVE A TEXT FROM JOHN, SO SHE just wrote it off as a no go and went back to work. She looked through the database and found everything she could about Charles Fisher. He had been employed as a casual fill in from 2018 but came on full time in January 2020. He got his certificate through a practicum at Pinkett's Funeral Home on East Dundas Street. Graduated U of T with a Bachelor's in History.

He was the only surviving family member from that murder in 2016 of the cop in High Park. She remembered the body; stabbed in the neck repeatedly when he opened the door to a tent that was unresponsive. He bled out instantly and died in minutes. The man in the tent was chased all over the park covered in blood and screaming that aliens were trying to abduct him. She remembered the wife's suicide shortly after that. She felt sorry for the kid; she knew how it felt to lose someone that close. When she lost her husband to cancer, she had thought of following him, but she could never do that to her daughters. She understood it though; that grief is all encompassing. *Charles' mom must have thought he would be better off without her,* she thought.

Amy hesitated suddenly. Should she really be doing this? Tracking this man. What if she was wrong? She sat back in her chair and paused. Just then her phone vibrated, it was John. Her hands began to shake as she set a meeting with him and closed her computer. If they tracked his movement and it turned out to be nothing, then nobody was hurt. If she was right, and it was him, she would have almost ignored the biggest motive in the world because she identified with him – that's not the job. The job requires facts and that is exactly what she was going to get.

John Sullivan sat on the front of his car looking out over the water on Lakeshore at the Port Credit Lighthouse. He sipped a coffee and watched the cars drive by as he waited for Amy. John had been doing surveillance for Toronto PD for 25 years. He was old school, and he knew it. The new tech didn't bother him, it just made things easier to record. Digital was a savior. He just sat back and worked half as hard for twice the money. He wasn't wearing his uniform; he looked like he was a tourist except that there were no tourists anymore.

When Amy pulled in, he stood up straight and exuded confidence for a second, and then he went back to slouching once she got out of the car, wearing a power-suit skirt with her hair up tight. He was outmatched.

I thought she said this was business, he thought.

"Just getting up?" she said in a sly tone.

"Just heading to the bar?" he snapped back.

"I thought you were in lockdown, all you government servants?" he said to recover.

"They let us out once in a while," she answered.

"Well, thank God for that," he replied.

"So, why I asked you here..." she said quickly to focus the conversation away from them, "is to get you to tail a young man who contracts for us moving bodies from the morgue.

"How bored are you guys?" he said with a laugh.

She smiled and said, "I need someone I can trust till we know what he is up to. Is that you?"

"Yes m'am," John said with a nod.

"Don't invoice me anything official. You know the drill; no emails or anything. I want it all on a stick," she said.

"What's new?" he said looking away.

Amy took a deep beath and swallowed hard before she said, "I need you on this one. It could be something big."

"I thought you were here to ask me about my divorce," he said looking down.

"I didn't know," she said surprised.

"Well, everyone else does... Left me for a taxidermist, believe it or not," he said embarrassed.

"Well, I'm sorry to hear about that," Amy said without thinking. She then reached in her purse and gave John the information. "Let me know if you find anything. I'll check back with you in a week if you don't contact me."

John raised the paper up in front of his face as he turned and walked to his car. Amy's ankles almost gave out as she walked back to the car, probably a mixture of the high heels that she never wore and butterflies from the unexpected reveal back there by John. She forgot how nice his eyes were: Hazel with a tint of honey, she used to say. John had that salt and pepper hair now, probably from the divorce. He had a son in college and a daughter in nursing school.

Must be bleeding him dry, she thought. *She would be there soon.* She watched his car disappear into the great beyond.

I hope he doesn't find anything, but only time will tell, she thought.

43

IT WAS A FRIDAY AT THE SITE, AND MIKAH WAS LOOKING FORWARD TO HER days off with Charles. She had come to rely on it as her salvation from a job that only took and barely replenished her energy levels. She felt like she was barely kept alive in that dark chamber where the sun did not shine, and the hours all felt the same. People shuffled in and out; cried and screamed; danced and dreamed, but at the end, she felt like she had nothing left to offer the world or herself. She needed those days off.

She looked at the computer screen and read articles about the month of April and its restrictions. She thought about what Perry had said about the conditions being the worst for this population. She had a spark of insight and she turned to Perry and said, "So, do we send a lot of people to treatment here?"

Perry looked around to see if anyone had heard her and then said, "Try to keep your voice down. This isn't the place for that sort of talk."

"Why?" Mikah asked.

"Do you remember what I said to you about agencies not talking to each other, which makes the job impossible to execute?" Perry asked.

"Yes," she answered.

"Well, the relationship between harm reduction and recovery is a perfect example of that. They hate each other," Perry answered.

"Oh, but why?" Mikah asked.

"Well, for one, they are competing for funding, which I mentioned to you before, and second, they are directly competing for hearts and minds. This means that there are many ways to see addiction services, but there can only be one winner. In the paper, they are starkly set against each other. The recovery people think that harm reduction is enabling the addict to continue using and not face the truth. Harm reduction people, like you and me, know the truth of the matter, which is: "You can't recover if you're dead."

We exist to right a wrong that was made a long time ago when recovery groups were invented. They have a $5 billion budget with a 3% success rate. We are here to keep people alive until we find a way to help them in a more permanent way. We are like the emergency room in a hospital. We triage for trauma, and then we send the people to the appropriate service within the hospital. Unfortunately, most never make it past the emergency room," Perry finished. He then stood up and patted his pockets for his smokes and looked back at Mikah.

"Plus, could you imagine Tdot at a meeting? Or K-ultra at a recovery house?" he said with a laugh. "Trust me, those boys have tried that. You couldn't be homeless if you hadn't tried," he scoffed.

"So, what's the answer?" Mikah asked.

Perry looked back at her and said, "The day we all stop pretending that we know what's best for people and listen to what the population is saying, the better off we will be," Perry said as he went outside.

Just then, out of the corner of her eye, she saw a participant named Rayleen tilt her head way back. Mikah stood quickly and went over to where she was and stood behind her, placing her hand on Rayleen's shoulder. She opened her eyes and leaned forward.

"Thanks," she said as she took a deep breath.

Mikah remembered her training and went back to her desk. She looked at the clock and thought about what Perry had said and loaded up another question for him. When he came back in and got set back in his position, she asked, "Why don't the meetings help these people?"

"Anyone want to answer that?" Perry asked the room. He was met with a couple groans, and one person said, "No."

He looked at Mikah and said, "Imagine Tdot, for instance, in a room full of people that need to be quiet while one person speaks. Imagine how high he would be. Now imagine the idea of abstinence. If the person needs to be high to take a shower, where would they be in terms of an abstinence-based, community? I'm not saying it can't be done. What I am saying is I understand why it's not done. We talk about lowering stigma around drug use. Recovered people are the worst offenders. They judge the harshest because they think if they quit, everyone can." He finished by clearing his throat and looking over at Rayleen.

"She's alright, I went over while you were gone," Mikah said anticipating his concern. Mikah went back in her head and recontextualized the new information, and then, defeated, she said, "I really don't know what we are doing here."

"We aren't here to save people; we are here to serve people. We are in the service industry," he said politely.

Mikah nodded her head in response to a saying she heard time and time again while working there. It was a hard urge to hold back; she constantly had to keep it in check. The need to know better and fix people came on strong for her. She was learning to get out of the way, slowly, all the time.

44

A WEEK HAD PASSED BY SINCE THEIR MEETING, AND AMY WAS ITCHING FOR some kind of update. All the old machinery from the affair was up and running in her mind, except there had been a great improvement since the last time. Guilt had been scrubbed off the mainframe. She was now operating with much less cynicism. She fired off a text early that morning:

Amy: You got that stick?

John: Is this sexting?

Amy: the zip drive.

John: sorry :(yes.

Amy: When can we meet?

John: Tonight? My place?

Amy didn't answer back for the rest of the morning. It was late afternoon when she finally texted him back.

Amy: See you @ 8

As Amy got ready for that night, she took a long time picking out what to wear. She went from a stern power suit to cute casual and back again. She hadn't been alone with a man in years, it seemed. She was nervous. She almost cancelled twice. She settled for cute casual but kept the hair up high. She headed out the door at 8:15.

When she got to his place, she inspected the cars outside to see what the situation was. His kids didn't seem to be there. She walked up the front step of the condo and knocked. She was met with a freshly shaved, over dressed man. He was wearing jeans and a button up polo

The Opiate Murders 2

shirt, untucked. He looked uncomfortable. When she saw this, she felt more comfortable.

"Hi," he said, as she stepped inside. She remembered all the sneaking around before and still felt apprehensive. "Do you want a drink?" he asked.

"Do you have wine?" she asked.

"Why yes I do. I just bought some," he said with a laugh.

She sat at the head of the table and pulled her laptop from her bag. "Let's see," she said extending her hand when he delivered the wine. He pulled a zip drive from his top breast pocket and placed it in the palm of her hand.

He began to talk as the images started to load. "We did a full search of all vehicles coming and going from the house, and we followed him on his routes both with GPS and two revolving tails," he said very official.

"Nothing right?" she said.

"Well, yes and no," he replied.

A pang went off in her stomach. "What do you mean?" she asked.

"Well, his driving between destinations doesn't deviate from the manifest. He is a machine, but one of these ambulances isn't registered," he said.

"Which one?" she asked.

"Scroll to image 57. That ambulance is steady; one drop per day at 1:30 a.m. It drives up to the house when he isn't there and drops off a body or two, and then leaves. We checked the database. There isn't anywhere that we know of that is deterring bodies to them. We checked all the other mortuaries in the city, and it doesn't deal with them either," he said.

"So where does it come from?" she asked.

"Well, it has some very interesting routes," he said, crossing his arms and standing behind her, looking over her shoulder.

She could feel him behind her, and a tingle went up the back of her neck. She could already feel him kissing her. She could smell his aftershave and took deep breaths as she looked at the screen.

"Where?" she asked trying to snap out of it.

"This ambulance doesn't take calls. It only drives around the city between Dundas and Queen Street East. It parks outside of different encampments," John said finally walking out from behind her and sitting down.

"What are they doing there," she asked.

"Well, it appears that they are responding to overdose calls, but then they don't go to the hospital, they go to the funeral home," he said.

"What?!" she almost screamed. Her mood went from erotic to panic instantly.

"Unless they have been directed away from the hospital because the body has COVID, I can't see why they would be doing it," John added. "I would have called this all in, but you told me to keep quiet," he finished.

"No, thank you. That's wild," she said, wiping the sweat from her forehead and closing the computer. She took a long deep gulp of the wine and stood. "I gotta go," she said.

"I know," he said standing up with her and following her to the door.

"Thanks for all your help," she said, hugging him with one arm and walking out to her car.

"Now that you know where we are, stop by anytime," she heard as she opened the door.

"Okay," she said as she lowered herself into her car. Her mind was racing a mile a minute. Who would she tell first? She didn't even know where to begin. She thought long and hard as she drove through the city, light after light. When she got home, she almost ran up the steps. She felt like a teenager. How could she be right? This was absolutely insane. It did make sense though. Nobody was watching, everyone is afraid at home. It's the perfect time to do something like this. You have an expected overdose death increase, and vulnerable population service shutdowns everywhere.

The situation was ripe for manipulation. She sat down at her computer and inserted the flash drive. Just then she thought of him and his smell and said to herself, "Not now," as she crossed her legs and leaned forward into the screen. She drafted an email to the mayor and the health authority. She asked for the funds, and the teams needed to coordinate the investigation. She sat back and watched the video surveillance and shook her head. *Unbelievable*, she thought.

45

DAX SAT IN HIS BEDROOM STARING DOWN AT A PARAMEDIC'S UNIFORM that was laying on his bed. He took a deep drag of his cigarette and exhaled the smoke up into the ceiling. He had been summoned. He was finally going to get his shot working on the river. He sat down on a chair in the corner of the room and cooked up a smash of crystal and heroin. As he injected the shot into his veins, his whole world got bigger and brighter. He was warm everywhere. The city was so cold all the time; he couldn't wait to smash. The cigarette burned away in his hand, and his eyes glistened with contentment.

This was what he was born to do, and he was going to show them all. The orange order was coming to a close with the end of April, and he was going to squeeze every last drop of death from the city that he could. He took a moment and held his pipe up to the light. He could see the souls floating inside. A tear came to his eye. *I wish I could come with you; my soul is tired and my bones ache,* he thought, putting the pipe back in his pocket. But the night was young, and there were lives to go before he slept.

46

MIKAH CAME TO CHARLES' HOUSE AT MIDNIGHT ON FRIDAY PREPARED FOR their trip. She had brought a few snacks with her and a thermos of coffee. They hopped into a black Econoline van with no windows and proceeded to drive down Dundas. "Okay, co-pilot, first we must go to the morgue and collect the first souls of the night," he said in an exhilarated tone.

She rose to meet it and thought, *This is going to be fun*, as she pushed down the fear she had previously carried with her. "I brought Krispy Kreme doughnuts and coffee," she said, her eyes glistening with excitement.

He smiled and drove contently, holding her hand the whole time. When they got to the morgue, he said, "Put all this PPE on. I'll be back in a minute," and he disappeared into the building.

Not even five minutes later, the large garage door opened, and Charles came out wheeling a stretcher with a black body bag on it. The back doors swung open, and Charles proceeded to slide the stretcher into the back of the van. He came around a moment later, jumped into the van, and started it. That was how the night went. Running back and forth between different funeral homes and the morgue.

"We have to drive up to Wellington County at 5:00. We will take our break there," he told her.

Charles was a machine. He seemed to know the city like the back of his hand, Mikah learned. Back alley after back alley between Queen Street and Dundas he navigated with ease. She was driven around to the back of churches and buildings she didn't realize were funeral homes or mortuaries. It was like a whole world of death and bereavement was hiding there in plain sight. She marveled at the speed and accuracy of Charles' job. He was so serious in his deliveries, but then so playful when they drove through the alley ways. He played the music and tapped on the dashboard. She sat back and watched him and felt that she knew him better than she thought she did.

At 4:30 a.m., he backed up to the garage doors at the morgue and shut the divider between the front and back so Mikah couldn't see. "These ones are COVID determents, so keep your mask on tight," he said as he went and collected two corpses and put them in the back. He slammed the back doors and then jumped up in the front. They stopped by his house quickly after that, and he came out carrying two bags that he put in the back. Before she knew it, they were on the road again. The night was still dark everywhere, but Mikah could see a glimmer of bluish orange on the horizon. It was the witching hour, and all the ghosts were headed back to bed.

47

AMY HAD COORDINATED WITH HOMICIDE, THE MAYOR'S OFFICE AND THE health authority. Homicide was tracking the ambulance everywhere it went. Turns out that during the day, the ambulance was being used to transport seniors all over the city to appointments. The van was owned and operated by a man that used to be a paramedic. He had bought the van cheap in an auction and kept it as is, obtaining a license to use it as a stretcher unit. Surveillance had tracked the ambulance at night, coming and going from different encampments. The van carried food and blankets to some encampments. To others it transported people and belongings. It wasn't until Saturday night that anything suspicious was reported. Homicide watched two paramedics get out of the van and collect a stretcher and head into a camp off Queen Street East.

48

DAX STEPPED OUT OF THE AMBULANCE, WALKING WITHOUT A CANE TO avoid any suspicion. He and his partner removed a stretcher and two air tanks from the back of the van. When they approached the park gate, they left the stretcher in the entrance to block anyone coming in. They moved quickly to their objective. Once outside the tent that had been previously scouted, they both knelt down and cut holes in the bottom of the tent silently. They slowly inserted hoses into each side of the tent and turned the cylinders to full. It would only take this mixture of carbon monoxide and pure fentanyl a couple of minutes to asphyxiate the couple inside, then they would bring in the stretcher and take the bodies.

Dax's heart was pounding. His eyes darted left and right, scanning the park, then in one brief moment everything changed. Lights lit up the park and a loud voice on an intercom yelled: "Stand up and put your hands on your head!"

Dax reached deep inside his uniform and pulled out a gun. He looked over at his associate and realized he didn't have one. Dax pointed the gun at his partner and pulled the trigger, shooting him in the head. Shots rained down on him as he scrambled to the outward fence. He fired in the direction of the flashes coming towards him but was shot several times as he made his way across the cold ground. He took deep breaths and kept moving. He was shot several more times in the back, which left him lying in a pool of his own blood, panting his last breaths. In that last moment, he was surrounded by the angels he had taken in his life. He felt a sense of purpose come over him in waves of euphoria, as he headed towards their beckoning call, and he closed his eyes.

49

"WHAT IS THIS PLACE?" MIKAH ASKED.

"I thought we could stop for a while, and I would show you one of my favorite places," Charles answered.

"What about them?" Mikah asked.

"They'll still be dead when we get back, don't worry," Charles said, getting out of his side of the van. When the two stepped out of the van, they stood in front of a large historical site with a very large white building with a spire on it. "This is the Wellington County Museum. They used to send Toronto's interned here," Charles said.

"Oh, I know this place. We studied it in school," Mikah said, rocking back and forth from her toes to her heels in excitement.

"Yeah, they used to send the poor and the destitute here to live, work, and die. You see the top floor there? That is where they used to sleep, and down on the first floor is where they would work, cook, and eat."

Mikah was excited to be doing something outdoors with Charles. She took a deep breath of the cool morning air and followed him off about six hundred yards to the side, down a ravine, and up a set of steps to what looked like a memorial site.

"This is the graveyard, where they have buried at least six hundred people here since the 1800s," he said, showing her the large, stand-up plaque with all the names and dates on it.

"Yeah, they used to intern people back then, not keep them in the city. They say that interning people could cure them of all sorts of things. Interning schizophrenics back then had a 93% success rate," Mikah said.

"Yeah, they stopped doing it because they invented pills. Now you have a crazy person on every street corner on six different kinds of meds," Charles said.

"I guess you see the camps constantly?" Mikah asked him.

"Yeah, the drugs have destroyed these people," Charles returned.

"In the Philippines they just kill the drug-addicted populations," Mikah added.

"Well, I could certainly understand that" Charles said. He stood there for a moment and stared down a path. "Did I ever tell you how my parents died?" he asked.

"Once," Mikah said, sitting down on one of the benches, watching him.

"When I was seventeen. You remember I said my dad was police?"

"Yes," she said.

"Well, one day, I guess, he was called to High Park, where a man was holed up in his tent and wasn't responding. When my dad opened the tent, the man attacked him and stabbed him to death. He ran all over the park covered in blood. There was this huge outcry for the man and how he needed proper medical supports. It's like my dad's life didn't matter," he said looking down.

Charles finally raised his head as Mikah approached him. "My mother slit her wrists in the bathtub while I was at a friend's house sometime after that."

Mikah almost stopped in her tracks at this. She nearly fell into him because her knees were so weak from hearing it. She held him for a moment and watched the sun rise. "I just wish that we had sent that man to somewhere like this," Charles said, patting her head and pulling away. "Something needs to be done about these people before they kill us all!"

Mikah looked up at him as he wiped his eyes, and she saw the diamonds in his eyes fading. His pupils had grown larger, when he said it.

"Yeah, we are definitely in a bad place," Mikah replied while rubbing his back.

"They used the place as a poor house until the 1920s and then it was turned into an old age home," he said changing the subject.

She admired how strong he was and that he could go through so much and still care about these people. She held his hand, and they walked back to the van through the trail. She pulled him to come down to her level, and she kissed his cheek. "Thanks for bringing me with you. I like going out with you," she said.

"Thanks for coming. I don't think anybody else would come on a date like this. Most people are terrified of COVID, homeless people, and dead bodies," he said.

"I think it's fascinating," she said turning crimson red with embarrassment. He looked at her in a way that she had never been looked at before. Like he understood, and it was okay. So many people nowadays were afraid of their own shadow, it seemed. It was nice to be with someone who welcomed it all. They got back in the van and drove down the highway after that. They had their whole lives ahead of them.

50

AMY PHONED JOHN THE NEXT MORNING WHEN SHE GOT UP. "HEY, HOW'D it go up there?" she asked.

"It's still going," he said.

"What do you mean?" she asked surprised. "They still haven't shown up yet," he answered.

"Seriously?" Amy said, scratching her head. She had expected it all to be over.

"Yeah, we tracked the kid out of the city, but then he stopped somewhere in Wellington. He has his girlfriend with him," John said.

"What!? What are you going to do?" she asked frantically.

"Take him when he shows up," John said nonchalantly.

She laughed to herself. How neurotic this must sound to a seasoned officer. "Okay, keep me posted," she said, as professionally as she could, and hung up. Her heart was pounding in her chest.

She called Ahmed a few minutes later to get her bearings. "Hey, what can you tell me about the shooters?" she said catching her breath.

"Well, they aren't going to make it," Ahmed said with a laugh.

Amy laughed too. "Okay, okay, I get it, but seriously…"

"This guy here with the limp was definitely doped up, track marks on his arms, a pipe on him, the works," Ahmed said.

"Keep the pipe, homicide is going to want that for prints and DNA. You remember that opiate murder investigation on the West Coast? They might be tied to that," Amy said.

"Okay, I'll keep you posted. Did they catch the guy?" Ahmed asked.

"Not yet. I'll keep you posted too. You might be busy today," she added.

"Too late!" Ahmed said.

51

CHARLES DROVE THE VAN INTO THE COMPOUND SLOWLY AS THE SUN WAS coming up. The light was penetrating the trees that surrounded the site with light beams through the branches. It got darker the farther they drove in. Once he got within a hundred feet of the lead building, five black cruisers approached him out of the darkness, and cars started to appear with lights flashing blue and red behind them.

Charles slammed on the breaks and stared intently at the flashing lights. He squeezed Mikah's hand and said, "I love you. I just wanted you to know that, and we will see each other again, somewhere across the river."

"What are you talking about? What's going on?" she yelled in a panic as she grabbed his forearm.

Charles grabbed an AR15 from behind him and kicked the door open. He opened fire on the police that were stationed beside the car and the ones in front. He was quickly riddled with bullets from behind, and he dropped to his knees. He looked up towards Mikah with blood coming out of the side of his mouth and exhaled panicked breaths before falling forward into the van's opened door and on to the seat, where he bled out.

Mikah was in shock. All she could hear was muffled screams as she was pulled from the van and carried away. She was handcuffed and placed in the backseat of a cop car, where she watched the drama unfold. The police cleared the weapon from Charles and checked his vitals before stepping away to search the van. Mikah watched the whole thing going on in front of her, but didn't believe it was real. She couldn't feel the tears running down her cheeks. She couldn't feel the life she once had leaving her body.

52

THE NEWSPAPERS CALLED IT A "MASSACRE IN WELLINGTON COUNTY". THE rest of the country focused on the cremated remains of hundreds of bodies, and counting, from what looked like cremated remains stuffed into the body bags of interred COVID victims. The county exhumed the site. Teams with hazmat suits pulled the remains of hundreds of bodies out of the communal graves. The county and the country were astonished by the findings.

Every place Charles had dealt with was thoroughly searched. Every known associate questioned, but they found no links to the Legion except the ambulance and what they had for surveillance. The trail was cold. Some would say that the bust was expected. Why else would the kid have an AR15 and a bag of ammunition with him in the van for a routine drop off? Amy scratched her head as she read the reports.

They were pulling DNA from bone fragments in the cremated remains trying to identify the bodies. Pinkett's was thoroughly cleaned every day, and the crematorium was no help for obvious reasons. This was a nightmare. No drugs were found at the Pinkett's home. All she had was a very shocked young woman waiting in a holding cell downtown.

The pipe on the paramedic had been linked to twelve overdose deaths over the last month. She was waiting on positive identification to come back on him from Vancouver. She sat back in her chair at the kitchen table of her house and was astonished by it all. In the days following Charles' death, there was a plague of overdoses. Many died but many were saved by the brave actions of paramedics and harm reduction workers both downtown and in the surrounding boroughs. Amy had one last statement to take.

53

MIKAH HAD BEEN ESCORTED BACK AND FORTH FROM HOLDING CELL TO interrogation room for weeks it seemed. It was always the same story; always the same insinuations that she was lying. She cried herself to sleep every night with the image of Charles scarred into her mind. She kept hearing his voice in her mind. It stayed with her. She loved him too. She wished she could have said it to him. She thought about his life often and tried to piece it together from the questions she was asked about him.

When she was led into the interrogation room for what felt like the millionth time, she was met with a strange site. Instead of two pit bulls waiting for her, there sat a woman, well dressed and beautiful even. It reminded Mikah of how horrible she must look. When Mikah came in the room, the cuffs were removed, and the woman slid a coffee over to her. Mikah took it gladly and took a large gulp of it.

"Hello, Mikah. My name is Amy Winter, and I'm with the Coroner's Office."

"Hi," Mikah said and nodded her head.

"I'm here today to talk about Charles, as you may already know," Amy said opening up her notes.

"Who else?" Mikah followed sarcastically. "Listen, I already told you people everything I know and don't know." Mikah finished.

"I'm not here for that. I'm here to talk to you about Charles' last day on this earth, where he went, what he thought about, even the music he was listening to," Amy said reassuringly.

"You guys collect that too?" Mikah asked sitting up confused. "Yes, we try and piece together the psychosocial aptitude of the deceased and ascertain his well-being. Was he happy? Was he focused?" Amy asked.

"Was he sane?" Mikah interjected.

"Precisely but not exclusively. We are interested in your interactions with him in that respect," Amy said writing something down and then looking up. "What do you know about him. Where did you meet?" Amy asked inquisitively.

"We met at the Tim Hortons across the street from my work," Mikah said after looking around the room and wiping her eyes that leaked all the time, it seemed.

"Did anything significant happen that day before or after?" Amy asked.

"It was the day of my first multiple overdose situation; two people died on the way to the hospital," Mikah said, taking a drink of the coffee.

"Did anything happen to you after that?" Amy asked.

"I started seeing overdose victims lying on the ground everywhere I went," Mikah said.

"Did you have any more situations at work like that?" Amy asked.

"No, as a matter of fact I didn't. Not even during the Hail Mary epidemic," Mikah said.

Amy sat back with a smile on her face.

"What?" Mikah looked across the table and began to get angry at the smirk on Amy's face.

"These guys have been doing this for a year. That is no coincidence," Amy said writing it down.

"What isn't?" Mikah asked forcefully.

"The lack of overdoses during your shifts compared to other people's. They seem to spike when you aren't there through the month of April. When did you meet?" Amy asked scribbling on her pad.

"Mid-March maybe," Mikah followed.

"It looks like he was protecting you," Amy said looking across the table. Mikah burst out into tears. Amy had to look away or she would have started to cry too.

"Did he tell you about his parents?" Amy asked.

"Yes," Mikah said wiping her eyes.

"This man could have been anything. I believe in my heart he was good. I just think that the grief transformed him into something he couldn't control," Amy stated.

Mikah stared at her for a long time after that and didn't say anything, until finally she looked over at Amy and said, "He was happy."

Amy nodded and said, "You'll be released soon. They can't connect you to anything. Thank you for your time." With that, she left the room, stopping only to take a picture in her mind of Mikah's face as she left. Mikah looked peaceful as she stared off into space.

Amy typed up her reports and filed what she could with the families of the missing people. It was a mess the city would never forget.

54

THE DOORBELL RANG AND JOHN STOOD UP TO FIND OUT WHO IT COULD BE. His kids were in town but at their mothers, so he was surprised by it. When he opened the door a very well-dressed Amy was standing on his stoop with a bottle of champagne in her hand.

"Well, well, well, I didn't expect to see you here," John said with a smile.

"Me either, but you looked so pitiful the other day when we met that I thought you could use a surprise," Amy said flashing him a very devious smile.

"Well, come on in," John said leading the way.

The door closed behind them, vanishing the light that shone from inside. A man sat across the street and lit a smoke. He would be following Amy from now on. New orders: Tie up any loose ends and try again. Death never sleeps.

THE END

CPSIA information can be obtained
at www.ICGtesting.com
Printed in the USA
BVHW032024120122
625846BV00008B/46

9 781039 130838